ALSO BY VINCENT N. SCIALO

The Rocking Chair

Randolph's Tale (A Journey for Love)

Deep in the Woods

Heigh-Ho

Not by Choice

Jesus (Journey Every Step Un-Sure)

The Decision

The Many Adventures of Grandpa and Grandpa's Girl

VACCINATED

Vincent N. Scialo

authorHOUSE®

AuthorHouse™
1663 Liberty Drive
Bloomington, IN 47403
www.authorhouse.com
Phone: 833-262-8899

Published by AuthorHouse 01/07/2022

ISBN: 978-1-6655-4772-7 (sc)
ISBN: 978-1-6655-4771-0 (e)

DEDICATION

Once again as done in my last eight books, I want to praise those who have continued to offer me guidance, strength and support.

To Jen, my wife and forever supporter. We have been through thick and thin and no matter what, you stand by my side. From the moment I saw you as a nerdy thirteen year old with my zipper pulled all the way up my parka, I was blinded by my love for you. You complete me and continue to complete our growing family.

To Marissa, Harry, Stephanie and Emma, you all mean the world to me. Living as close as we do makes life all the more enjoyable and I love every minute I can spend with each of you.

To Jeff, my ambitious son. Keep on striving and chasing that dream. Remember that dreams really do come true!

To Michele Ronzo who took the time to read and critique this novel. And for your constant pushing me to move it along with no stopping or time for writer's block. Thank you, thank you, thank you!

To Cristen Ronzo-Marcy, for the editing of this book which is never an easy task.

To CHRISTOPHER Zappia, for your cover design and friendship. You LIVED!

And lastly to my faithful readers who continually enjoy my novels and inspire me to once again take pen to paper or shall I say fingers to keyboard.

ENJOY the story!

CONTENTS

NEW YEAR'S DAY

Life was anything but new for the first day of January. Since last March, the whole world had been shut down from the pandemic, which still hadn't been given a proper name. Some countries were calling it the next black plaque. Others, the inhumane strain. Here in the good ole USA though it was referred to as the Rapid X virus. Rioters were taking advantage of businesses shut down and were pilgrimaging the stores of their entire inventories. The police forces throughout the country didn't have the manpower to stop the influx of destruction in the major cities. The number of cases of the virus had lessened their task forces by almost half. With close to 100 million people infected and over 27 million deaths, there was mass panic in the United States. With the total US population at 340 million Americans, that number of deaths was crucial. Even the President and his cabinet were not able to calm down the nation. His most recent Presidential Address left the nation feeling hopeless. Without any type of cure in the near future, people from every state were taking matters into their own hands. Supermarkets couldn't stock the shelves fast enough due to supply and demand and others were selfishly taking more than what was needed as if this was the apocalypse. Most government offices were operating with a minimal staff. All schools and universities were closed until further notice, and children were being home schooled. To make matters worse, many people were either laid off or working from home, making the situations at home unbearable for most. The economy and stock market were the worst in American history, and the unemployment rate was at an all-time high. Foreclosures had quadrupled in the past year. Even most of the banks weren't approving loans since there was a lack of money circulating around the country. Hospitals weren't able to keep up with the overload of patients and had temporary tents set up in their parking lots to accommodate the overload. Along the eastern and western seaboards, Navy carriers were docked and being used as treatment centers as well. The morgues were at their highest capacity, and trucks with freezers were brought in to store the bodies. Currently, no funeral services were being allowed in order to contain the spread. The dead were being buried and cremated as fast as time would allow. Families were left in total shock without a chance to say their final goodbyes. Many of the dead died by themselves in various hospitals as family members were not permitted entrance into them. The country was crumbling and fast. The President had ordered the National Guard to patrol the streets in order to maintain the curfew and even to assist in the removal of the bodies from homes. The 911 call operators were inundated with neighbors informing the police of the strong odors coming from the decaying dead left unattended in houses on their streets. Massive panic was a daily occurrence as people were unable to live their normal lives.

Ingrid Birnbaum woke up on New Year's Day with the hope of this day being the start of a better year. Having lived alone with only the assistance of a daily aide Monday through Friday from nine to five provided her with just the right amount of care. After she lost her husband of sixty-four years twelve years ago, Ingrid still lived in the house where she raised her only son, Jonathan. Jonathan was sixty-three and married to his high school sweetheart for the past forty years. Their three grown children and their children's eight children made for a very fulfilling life for Ingrid. She still lived on the same block where all her children were born and raised. Ingrid and her husband made their house a home in Rhode Island. She counted her blessings as no one in her family succumbed to the deadly virus. Today was her hundredth birthday, and she could never have imagined living as long as she has to become a centenarian. Her children had planned something simple, as most establishments were closed or forced to close from lack of business. At first, she was too afraid to venture outdoors in fear of the unknown, but having been the first group selected to be vaccinated put her mind at ease. The CDC had issued a mandatory vaccination for all Americans. There was no getting around the vaccination regardless of your health, wealth or mental state. To ensure this requirement was met, the everyday function to exist in the world required this to be performed. To travel, attend school, receive medical assistance and even grocery shopping meant you needed to show proof of your vaccination. In order to guarantee this was performed, a permanent star was tattooed on the left inside of the tip of a person's pinky. You needed to place your pinky on a scanner where all your pertinent information, along with a photo, proved your inoculation. Each and every state set up temporary borders to prevent any form of transportation amongst states. Citizens throughout the country were up in arms from being forced to follow these protocols until people started dying faster than imaginable. Most Americans abided by these rules administered to them. Sixty percent of the world's current population had been given an antidote to kill Rapid X. The other forty percent were broken up as follows: Twenty percent of the world had succumbed to the virus, and ten percent were children under five, who didn't seem affected by this pandemic. The other ten percent hadn't been accounted for since many variables came into play in tracking them down. Soon after the outbreak, many people fled to various parts of the world. Rumors circulated that communities were developed in hidden parts of the world, hoping that one day the world would go back to the normal they once knew. Until then, your safest bet was to abide by current laws. Ingrid didn't see much harm in spending the afternoon at the nearby park with a picnic lunch that her family had insisted they do outdoors where the air was fresh and clean. Eating outside would provide the whole family a sense of comfort under the current circumstances. Dressed in her Sunday best of her favorite floral pattern, Ingrid slowly stood up from her recliner after hearing the doorbell ring. As usual her kids were prompt. They had set the time for noon and it was eleven-fifty-eight. Ingrid could hear voices and laughter from the other side of her front door. Since it was such a clear and sunny day she had her curtains pulled back to allow the sunshine in. Gathered on her front steps, she caught a quick glimpse of most of her family. She couldn't place their faces as balloons and presents obstructed her view. Packages and presents so decorated it made her smile. The amount of balloons made her giggle as she imagined herself a young girl again pretending they would lift her off the ground. The doorbell kept ringing as she pictured some of the younger great-grandchildren pushing against one another to press the bell. Ingrid placed her hand on the doorknob just as her grandfather's clock in the living room struck twelve noon. The first chime of the other eleven to follow always sounded pleasing to her ears. Ingrid was the happiest she felt in quite a while. And as she went to open the door to the sounds of laughter and well-wishes, Ingrid dropped dead right there on the floor.

~~~~~

All around the world cellphones dialed into their respective emergency phone numbers to report the sudden death of a loved one, neighbor, or a person they came across outside. The volume of phone calls eventually overloaded most cell towers and calls were no longer capable of going through. Hysteria was in full overload and people were scrambling to the relative safety of their homes. Reports were coming in confirming that almost every casualty was a victim over the age of one hundred. Drastic events had taken place all around the globe. Car accidents caused major pile ups because a centenarian driving behind the wheel of his or her automobile simply died and swerved out of control. In doing so, cars collided, crashed and careened into any object that crossed their paths. News media outlets were trying to calm the general public into believing that a supernatural phenomenon had taken place causing anyone one hundred years of age or older to perish. This was not a calming effect and only raised the tension level of almost every human being able to understand the magnitude of this catastrophe. Citizens all over the world expressed outrage, confusion, and a need for a more definitive answer. It appeared the moment of death for all of these individuals occurred at exactly the same moment in time. It was estimated that at least one percent of the world's population had succumbed to this untimely death. An exact number of casualties could take weeks to determine. Numbers from every country and continent were streaming in as each government did their best to report accurate numbers. Having just suffered and survived the worst pandemic to ever occur, this additional burden struck a chord close to every human heart. Just when people's spirits were resurfacing, a blow of this kind set them back to day one of the worst virus mankind had ever experienced. In barely the time it took to realize that a tragedy of this proportion was underway, within the next twenty-four hours any individual ninety-nine years of age soon met the same demise. At precisely the same time of the previous day, the exact same scenario took place once again. Phone lines were once again jammed, this time at a faster pace than the day before.

1

One Week Prior

In a remote cabin on the outskirts of Shandaken Township, Peter Palumbo double checked to make sure all of his windows and both the front and back door of his house were locked. Living at 29 Timber Lake Road was the farthest place The Organization would look for him. Still, Peter felt completely on edge. It had been over five weeks since he fled the building in the middle of the night. His shift wasn't over until 7pm that evening, but he managed to flee during his hour- long break. Harry and Darryl were completely unaware of his agenda when he told them he was stepping outside for a smoke. The Organization strictly prohibited smoking on the premises, but with the urgency and pressure they were under, neither of them questioned his whereabouts. Lately, most employees dealt with the daily pressure in their own ways. The restrictions they were forced to follow didn't allow them much free time. When

Peter joined the company, he was just an intern straight out of college. For the first five years, he basically went from department to department fulfilling most other employees' needs. In such a short time he became intrinsic to the company's future. Under the guidance of Doctor Walter Anglim (pronounced Ann-Glim), he took Peter under his wing and taught him the true nature of the beast. The beast being what was now underway to contain the pandemic virus and the future of civilization. Doctor Anglim had been closely monitoring Peter's work ethics the past few years. He seemed like a young man who could be trusted, and trust was of utmost importance to what The Organization, led by the doctor, had in mind. Since the pandemic was spiraling out of control, this was the perfect opportunity to put their plan into effect. An arrangement that was caused by something which they thought was trivial at first, now proved differently. A master plan to rid the world of the general population and leave only the superior was long overdue. Bringing Peter on board took some convincing to the higher authorities. Dr. Anglim had prepared a presentation which documented and highlighted all the attributes that Peter had performed. Once convinced of how Peter could benefit the project, the elite board of directors agreed and shook hands with Dr. Anglim, cementing their agreement. An agreement that sped up faster than anticipated. Again, this all happened so rapidly within the past year that Peter barely had time to register what was actually taking place. All he knew was that over 27 million US citizens had perished from the outbreak in the past twelve months. No one in any capacity of government or the medical field was prepared for such a fast moving virus. What was brought over from Europe from an unspecified tourist area in either Germany or Italy, was as close as they were to pinpointing its origin. Several Americans that were on the same flight were the first to contract the deadly virus upon returning to the United States. Two hundred and forty people were on that deadly flight from all areas of the country. The initial spreading of the pandemic had reached seventeen of the fifty states within the first four days of the contagious flight.

Now, at age twenty-nine and just a few months short of his thirtieth birthday, Peter was a hunted man. There were quite a few close calls when he thought this was it. He would be taken, bound, and most likely killed within a few hours of his capture. Peter had and knew too much information that would destroy The Organization he once was so proud to say he was employed by. Since he fled, Peter dyed his hair from a sandy blonde to a dark brown. Weeks prior he had ordered online contacts to change his sparkling green eyes to a vivid brown. His grandparents were both from Campania, Italy, just north of Naples. Many of his ancestors were of lighter hair coloring and light eyes. In fact, Peter was named after his father's father which was very common in Italian tradition. His parent's changed the spelling of his name from Pietro to make it sound more Americanized. They didn't want him growing up sounding like he came right "off the boat". His middle name was Nicholas after his own father. He had hoped with this new disguise he could lessen his chances of being recognized by the many people hunting him down. In an all-out effort to put distance between the newly considered "bad guys". Peter even resorted to cutting his shaggy hair, which he kept tied in a longer than usual ponytail, to shoulder length. This was a drastic measure that was necessary to alter his appearance. After all, if he was able to avoid his capture, his hair was the least of his worries. Unfortunately at 6'4" his height was a hindrance. He could easily be spotted over the average height of most individuals. At least he was in shape, weighing roughly 180 pounds which made it easier to bounce around undetected. Getting the information he had into the right hands was of utmost urgency. How he was going to accomplish this was beyond him. What, where, and how needed to be sooner than later if the rest of humanity was to be saved. If not, mankind would be wiped out in less than a few days, come the first of the New Year. Peter went over to the safe he kept hidden in the second bedroom of the upstate house he purchased just over six months ago with anticipation of what was to come. This was by far his wisest decision to date. The second wisest decision was how he would stop this pandemic from eliminating every man, woman, and child in the whole world. Peter opened the safe and reached in to touch what he had done every day for the last 35 days since he stole what could quite possibly save humanity. His hand shook as he held the tiny vial and looked at the small amount of liquid that, if administered correctly, could reverse the damage of the original vaccination. Locked away were hundreds of thousands of the antidote. If distributed in equal amounts, at least half if not most of the population might have a chance. The only solution is who would be able to survive long enough to beat the odds. Peter, having never been a gambler, didn't think winning this battle was in his favor, but he was willing to die trying, and as for now, getting to the White House was his ultimate mission. Whether he made it there dead or alive was the question.

2

Sitting at the head of the conference table surrounded by some of the country's most dignified scientists and prestigious doctors, Dr. Anglim took in a deep breath then slowly released it before he spoke. "Gentlemen and Ladies, it saddens me to say that Mr. Palumbo has since not been located as of yet. We have the most trained teams searching every possible inch of the state of New York." Dr. Anglim glanced at each face currently present within the room. Having just turned seventy-one this past year, he felt his best in years. With daily workouts which consisted of cardio and strength training, Dr. Anglim looked ten years younger than his age. He maintained the same weight for years regardless of his large quantities of food consumption. His brown hair was graying at the temples and standing at a mere five foot eight inches, his presence rather on the short side, still he loomed larger when he entered a room. Starting Epigen Hyperspace Inc. over forty years ago was his greatest accomplishment. Having the world's most renowned scientific leaders on board made this all the more possible. This was not an easy task for Dr. Anglim at first. Convincing fellow scientists his plan to eliminate most of mankind so that only the elite would rule the earth, came with exhausting measures. Documentation to his ultimate plan and the many appeals to only those he deemed worthy, wore heavily upon him. His first scientist to join forces with him came from Italy. Flying across to Italy and meeting his first potential comrade gave the doctor hope; hope that his plan would pan out in due time. Little did he realize that his Italian scientist was a much-respected man in his profession and was able to bring three other scientists from other countries to agree to the annihilation of humanity. With the United States, Italy, Germany, Austria and Switzerland all for this plan, getting other countries should be an easier task.

3

"Tommy stop! Just listen to what I'm saying. I don't have much time to tell you what I need from you. You HAVE to get Mom, Dad, and Maya away from our house. Do you hear me? Right away! Don't waste any time. Pack a few bags and leave!" Peter shouted into the phone, barely catching his breath. Tommy stood in his parents' kitchen on his cell phone looking out the window into the backyard. He was certain he saw figures moving among the bushes toward the fence in the back. The past two days they noticed unusual activity around their house as they came and went about their business. Having not heard from his brother Peter for the past week kept his family on edge, knowing something of grave danger was lurking close to home. Looking nothing alike and five years younger, Tommy was two inches sort of six feet. He was built more muscular and had a darker complexion with brown buzzed cut hair and eyes the color of midnight. Whenever they were together the two brothers had to convince most of their bloodline since the similarities were far and few between. Hearing the concern in his brother's voice made him listen more attentively before replying, "I hear ya bro! Slow down. You're babbling and you're scaring me. Why the urgency and what the hell is going on? You just disappeared off the planet and you left mom and dad worried sick. You missed Christmas Eve and Christmas. Mom's favorite holiday of the year and not a beep from you. It was just another day for all of us. Pop kept calling Epigen Hyperspace and got nothing but the runaround, as if you disappeared off the face of the earth. Not a single soul returned his calls and those who answered provided him with squat. Dr. Anglim was nowhere to be found and didn't have the decency to return at least a dozen or more voicemails pleading for any information regarding your whereabouts. Now you're calling half winded barking out ridiculous demands that are near impossible. There are strange people lurking all around the house day and night. We can't leave the house without feeling like we are being watched. Is this because of..."

Interrupting his brother mid-sentence, Pete frantically continued, "I'm certain it is! They've been tracking me down the past week and I managed to slip past them to a remote spot they haven't been able to detect yet. I'm on a burner phone so this call can't be traced and I feel as if they are hot on my trail. These are BAD people. Very bad people capable of doing unmistakable things to keep their secret safe. Even if murdering my whole family to get to me. They'll stop at nothing! You need to leave College Point and we can meet up at the spot mom and dad took us to every summer. Don't say a word about its location. I can meet you there at the crack of dawn. I'll come to you. Just park in the lot. You drive and don't tell mom or dad a word of this conversation. Do you understand me? Tell them it's imperative to leave as soon as we hang up."

"What? Listen to yourself! Are you mad or plain right crazy? You want me to hang up, pack our essential belongings and just tell mom and dad we're going on a field trip. Are you for fucking real bro? We've been racking our brains as to where you went and even if you were still alive the past few weeks and out of the blue you want to turn our lives upside down. And what do I tell Maya? She's been crying almost day and night worried sick not hearing from you. She's your girlfriend for Christ sakes! She lives with us. She has no family here in the states. Her parents and siblings are miles away living in Bermuda. You're all she's got and you leave no note, nothing and now I have to convince three people who love you dearly of your mad plan."

"I get it! I do Tommy. I really do. But please, please trust me on this," Pete pleaded exasperated.

"I do. I would never doubt you bro. I just don't know how to go about it. How do I explain to mom and dad and Maya with little to no information? What if those people are outside watching the house? How do we just load the car and drive off on our merry way? What if they stop us and won't let us leave?"

"Tell them that they need to follow along and get as far away from the house as possible while there's still time. I guarantee in the next couple of days, they'll be no longer leaving once the shit hits the fan. It's nine o'clock. That gives you almost ten hours to devise a family plan, pack up and escape the neighborhood unnoticed. The drive to our spot shouldn't take more than two to two and a half hours at most to meet at sunrise. You can do this! You'll think of something. You were always good at conjuring up a story. Well make this one your best one yet. I know you can," Pete pleaded to his younger brother.

After getting an earful of what Tommy sensed as a fore-warning of what could eventually happen, he took a slow steady breath before finally giving his brother what he needed to hear most at this very moment, "I got your back bro. Always have and always will. Don't you worry about me, I'll get us there one way or another. I can guarantee you that!"

4

Having entered the kitchen from the living room after Tommy had raised his voice, Rita, Peter's mom, spoke first after Tommy hung up. "Do you mind telling us what exactly is going on? Seriously, after what? Close to five weeks later Pietro finally calls. Let us believe he's dead. What kind of crap is that?" At fifty-seven years old she still looked like she could pass for someone in her late forties. At 5'8" and a mere one hundred and fifteen pounds, Rita still had heads turned when she walked past a group of men. Pietro, as she liked to refer to Peter as, took after his mother with the lighter hair and eyes. Rita's eyes were a lighter blue reflecting more of a crystal clear sky on a perfectly sunny day. Nicholas, Pietro's father chimed in too before giving Tommy the chance to answer his mom's questions. "Wait until I get my hands on that boy. Having us worried sick these past few weeks. Look at your mother. I haven't seen her this distraught since 9/11. A parent's worst nightmare is losing your kid and he just disappears with no contact. My own father would have kicked my ass if I pulled that shit at his age." Standing the exact same height as Tommy with the similar build as his younger son, Nicholas didn't take after the lighter eyes and hair color of his Italian ancestors. Peter was more like his parents in looks than he was coming from his town in Italy. Staring at Tommy with his piercing brown eyes, he waited for an explanation.

"According to Pete, some serious shit is going down. He fled from Epigen during his shift in the middle of the night. It has something to do with a secret and killing anyone in their way to keep it that secret. Including us." Rita gasped, covering her mouth with one hand. Nicholas walked over to Rita and put his hand in hers. Maya, who was up in her room she shared with Pete, just happened to come downstairs to grab a coke, saw the three of them in the kitchen, and looked at them quizzically. "Sorry, I didn't mean to interrupt. I thought at this point I would be included in all family meetings. I can leave if you want me to?" She felt awkward at the moment. The three of them moved aside to make her feel more welcomed. If at all, she was now an integral part of the Palumbo family. Maya first met Pete when they both worked at the Starbucks in the neighborhood. Maya was instantly taken by Pete's good looks, and she let the other girls know to lay off her soon to be man. Twenty-two at the time and right out of St. John's College, she was eager to date and have a relationship rather than pursue her law degree in criminal justice. Pete, on the other hand, worked only two afternoons a week, to be around peers more his age than at the laboratory. He was banking most of that money to purchase his own home by his thirtieth birthday. One day during his shift, Peter noticed Maya sobbing in the breakroom. Noticing no one else was around and seeing her cry uncontrollably, he felt he needed to ask how he could help. Considering she was the most attractive girl who worked there, made it all the more desirable to assist. At 5'4" she was almost a full foot shorter than him. Not knowing her background, he gathered she was half Caucasian and later learned her father was born in Bermuda. Her skin complexion was of a lighter color, more so than her father's darker coloring. He was a natural citizen of the island, and he met her mother while she was vacationing on a cruise ship that was docked for two days. It was on one of the excursions from her cruise ship when they bumped into one another. They instantly fell in love and married, and he was currently working off a temporary extended visa in the states. She was one of four siblings and a twin herself. On the day of her heartache, her parents informed her that he was promoted to VP of the largest bank currently in Bermuda. There were far too many VP's in different branches of the bank throughout the tristate area. The bank had a suitable location more desirable from his native island and being a citizen of Bermuda sealed the deal. Besides, with the cost of living so expensive in New York, her parents thought a change of lifestyle was in order. The promotion also covered relocation costs. Additionally and fortunately for them, he still had family there making the transition that much more appealing. Maya was so invested in her education that she wasn't prepared to leave, but they were insistent she make the move with them. Contemplating how she would not have to leave the only place she knew as home devastated her. Now, as she bawled her eyes out, she didn't even realize that someone much taller was standing over her with what appeared to be a tissue in his hand. Peter gently wiped the tear running down her cheek as he noticed for the first time just how beautiful her hazel eyes were. Her dream of making this young guy fall for her had only just begun. It was from that moment forward that they spent as much time as possible getting to know each other, which resulted in them now living together in Peter's parents' home for the past five years. A decision never had to be made for her to move with her family to Bermuda when the time had finally arrived. Each of them was head over heels for one another, and convincing Peter's mom and dad to let them live together instead of her moving out of the country was never even an issue. So now, as she faced the other three people who also meant the world to Peter in the kitchen, she waited to be invited to join in.

Maya sounded exasperated. "Now as in right now? How do we know what's going on when you're being so vague? A secret that can get us all killed if we find out what it is, and to just pack our bare essentials and leave ASAP. Tommy, you have to let on as to what is the real purpose behind this."

"I told you all I can. I promised Peter I would do as he wanted. You have to trust him on this."

"And when and how long until we come back here? Will we even come back here?" Rita asked with a quiver in her voice. Nicholas, who had been silently absorbing most of the current conversation, finally joined in, "Sweetheart, for Pietro to call after not hearing a word from him in quite some time, sounds like this is serious business. From his brief exchange with Tommy we need to do as he wishes. No use wasting time with all the what ifs."

"I'm just scared and not knowing what is in store frightens me even more," Rita tried to explain, still in her shaky voice.

"I agree. What if whoever wants to keep this powerful secret follows us when we leave the house? What do we do then?" Maya questioned.

Tommy wasted no time in replying, while trying to ease their minds in the process. "I'll leave out the front door in hopes that will distract whoever might be watching us. While I think of something to draw their attention to me and away from you three, Pop will get the car out from the garage and slowly drive off, hopefully unnoticed. I'll jump some backyard fences and meet you at the Dunkin Donuts on the corner of 112th street and Magnolia Ave. Shouldn't take me more than ten to fifteen minutes tops. I just have to think up some sort of distraction that will give me that extra time."

Together, the four of them each packed a suitcase, while Rita and Maya also stocked a duffle bag with cans of food and non-perishables from the fridge. While Nicholas loaded the car in the garage with what they had gathered, Tommy searched until he found what he was looking for. Nicholas always kept a five-gallon gas can filled in case any of them ever ran out of gas. In all of their years of marriage, Rita only once let the gas gauge run until it was empty. It was in their early years of being married before the boys were born. It was an ordeal to get to the gas station and finally to the car to refill the tank to get her home. Since then Nicholas, more out of habit than anything else, always had gasoline on hand for just such an emergency.

Tommy, with the gas can in hand, ran back into the kitchen pulling open some drawers until he found what he was looking for. The extra-long Bic lighter they used to start the grill outside for barbecues, was the only other thing needed to go forth with his plan. After kissing both his parents on the cheeks, Tommy exited the garage from the side door and fled into the darkness of the night.

Nicholas, Rita and Maya left their cellphones in a different room in the house and quietly tiptoed into the garage. It had been thirty minutes since Tommy had left them. After quickly explaining his plan, he instructed them to wait until they heard the fire sirens heading in their direction. Once the fire engines passed down their blocks, he wanted them to wait a full five minutes before opening the garage doors to back out.

~

Tommy slowly crept in the shadows of each house along the block. He didn't want to be spotted, and in his black hoodie and sweatpants he blended in quite well. Careful not to alert any of his neighbors, he inched his way along until he came upon his ultimate destination. The tall oak stood in the center of the block far away from the other houses. It stood between two homes at the base of their driveways, enough distance away as to not catch fire to anything nearby. Tommy poured the entire five gallons of gas up, down, and all around the tree. After he poured the last bit of gas out of the can, he reached into his pocket and pulled out the lighter. As the lighter blazed from the flick of his finger, Tommy lit the handkerchief he stuffed into his other pocket. Once the white material caught fire, he flung the flaming piece of cloth at the bottom of the tree. Instantly, the flames ignited the gasoline and within seconds the entire tree was on fire. The brightness lit up the whole area. Within seconds a bedroom light from a nearby house turned on. Tommy tucked behind a car while holding his breath. Counting down from fifty, his prayers were answered. Off in the distance he heard the first of what he was sure would be many sirens. Front doors were opening as he quietly listened. Tommy unintentionally smiled, knowing his plan so far was working. Running towards the fire were what sounded like footsteps. Footsteps he was positive belonged to the enemies Peter had warned him about. Tommy knew he only had a mere few seconds before the possibility of being spotted. So, as Tommy held his breath, he slithered away like a snake in the grass and headed for the Dunkin Donuts.

5

The sun had barely risen when Tommy, along with his parents and Maya, pulled into the parking lot off of Route 28 near Shandenken. Peter was standing outside of a car Tommy didn't recognize. It was apparent that his brother had somehow managed to steal the car in his escape. Tommy had stepped on the brake and hadn't even put the car in park when Maya jumped out the back door and ran straight into Peter's arms. Next, his parents exited the vehicle and joined in with tears of joy and relief that their older son was safe and sound. Soon after as Tommy shut the car off and walked over, Peter tousled his brother's hair and gave him a fierce hug showing his affection for a job well done.

Nicholas, his father, shed tears of joy and moments later changed his tone of voice. "And just what the hell kept you from calling your mother? She was worried sick and cried herself to sleep every night. If I wasn't so happy to see you alive I would kill you myself." He said this knowing fully well he never had intentions of any kind.

"Pop, forgive me, but this is bigger than big. It's only going to get worse. Every day until the youngest age, the whole of civilization will become extinct."

Baffled and confused, the four of them just stood there staring at Pietro.

"I know you don't understand, and trust me none of this makes any sense but this is what will happen. Within the next 30 days, not one single soul will be alive. Only the few who masterminded this extinction will still be breathing."

Tommy shook his head, "So what you're saying is that all of mankind, including us, will die on a given day?"

"Precisely! Let's get back to the cabin and I'll explain exactly how, what, when and everything else there is to make you completely aware of this madness. I'm just hoping I, well, we can stop it before it's too late. It's best if we leave your car here and all pile in this one. They could already have put a trace on our car using your license plates."

As all five of them piled into the stolen car heading to the hidden cabin in the woods, others were at work to finalize plans that they hoped would eliminate the enemy.

6

As Dr. Anglim headed the Zoom conference call to various countries at different hours of the day, all eyes and ears were focused on his precise words. "At approximately 0700 hundred hours we will have terminated the major problem at hand and continue with our twelve noon extinction. I have instructed our terminators to detonate the explosives as soon as the sun rises above the mountains. We are just minutes shy of this taking place."

All the other cabinet members from various countries applauded the doctor as he finished speaking. They, too, were overjoyed to proceed with their plan without any further interruptions.

⁓

Peter was driving around the last bend before heading up the long dirt road that served as a driveway to the cabin. He lowered his car visor as the glare from the sun just rising over the mountain reflected off the windshield. Once they were all in the safety of the cabin he would tell them in detail exactly what his plans were. As he slowed the car to avoid the many potholes in the road, it may have been a frustrated inconvenience that just saved their lives.

Dr. Anglim checked his watch. It was 0659 hours and thirty seconds. His thumb clicked the text to be sent to his contacts to eliminate his once most favorite person in his world to his now most hated. In a mere half of a minute there would no longer be a loved or hated individual that existed in his world.

The entire structure of the small cabin had been wired within the last three nights while Peter was unaware of what took place. These hired professionals were so clever and as quiet as mice to go unnoticed among the surroundings of the cabin. The wires ran along the complete structure of the outside and were joined together and run to a box that would serve as the detonator. A detonator, frequently a blasting cap, is a device used to trigger an explosive device. As the three hitmen counted down from ten as if they were celebrating ringing in the New Year, little did they know that their intended target was not where he was supposed to be. With pure joy in their eyes and excitement in their blood, the ringleader pressed down on the handle with complete astonishment. What had once been a place of residence was now blown to pieces in seconds. Rubbing his hands together, he smiled to his two other cohorts for what he considered a job well done.

Maya was the first to scream out. Peter swerved the car and almost went completely off the road. His mother, Rita, cried out and made the sign of the cross from the back seat next to Maya. Nicholas reached out to grab his son Pietro by the shoulders to reassure him that he made the right move. Seated next to him, Tommy cursed without realizing, "What the fuck? What the fuck just happened?" Reaching over and swatting the back of his head, Rita still shell shocked, yelled, "Watch your language young man or you'll get more than a swat next time."

With her hand over her heart it appeared as if she herself was having a heart attack. Maya was now sobbing uncontrollably. Peter hushed her as he tried to make heads or tails as to what just happened, as he witnessed his hideaway blown to smithereens.

~

"I knew it! I just knew it! That's why I parked this car half a mile away. Something told me that I wasn't safe. I snuck out the back porch door and stomach crawled along the ground until I was a safe distance away. Come to think of it, I thought I heard some rustling not too far from me in one of the bushes, making me even more cautious. I'm almost positive that if I didn't dress in all black I would have been spotted. How the hell did they track me to this cabin so fast? Now look at this shit. If we were a few minutes early we……" He stopped without saying what they all knew.

Trying to stay focused and remain calm, Peter managed to turn the car in the direction heading away from the rubble. Pieces of the cabin landed on the car but not enough to do serious damage. All that was left as Pietro peered in the rearview mirror were flames that resembled the pits of hell ablaze in the early morning light. As he accelerated at a safe speed to not break an axle, the five occupants of the vehicle stared in amazement at what could have been. As to where they were headed no one knew, but deep in the mountains seemed their safest bet.

7

Dr. Walter Anglim had the biggest smile spread across his face as he watched the cabin explode into a million little pieces. For this late in December, it was a very mild winter especially for upstate New York. With little to no snow on the ground, the flames burned brighter than the sunrise. Satisfaction guaranteed was all that went through his mind. A job well done. He was more than willing to pay the extraordinary payoff needed to complete this mission. As soon as the banks opened, he would wire transfer the money to the offshore accounts associated with the three buffoons who did the job. They came highly recommended and were true professionals known to keep the secrets just as they were, secretive. As he ended the Zoom call with high regards and congratulatory praises, he felt better than he had in days. In fact he felt like he was on top of the world. Today was going to be his best day yet. The only factor that he never saw coming, was that in less than thirty minutes his complete happiness was about to turn sour. A taste so bitter, he might never recover.

8

"What? How? Didn't you have the whole cabin under surveillance? I paid you to do a job for Christ sakes!" Dr. Anglim's voice got louder as he felt his face flush from the madness taking control of him.

"No, no, no…don't hand me this bullshit. You were given one simple task and you blew it. Unfortunately you blew up the mission as well as the cabin. Now you tell me you saw a car with four or five people driving toward the cabin just as it exploded. And to top it off, the driver was Peter himself. Why didn't you stop the car and kill them all?"

Walter Anglim listened to the man in charge apologize with excuse after excuse. Nothing he said mattered as far as he was concerned. They failed in their attempt to eliminate the enemy, and now it sounded as if his family was with him. They, too, were under 24/7 surveillance. How in God's name did they also manage to flee their home?

None of this was making sense or for that matter working to his advantage. At this point all the loose ends were to be neatly tied up. Now all the ties were unraveling and spinning out of control. He needed to start from scratch, and his time was extremely limited, with his next few steps to proceed with the extinction of mankind. Plus he would have to alert all the leaders of the other countries who were on the Zoom call as to the failed attempt. This would make him look incompetent and that was something he would not tolerate. He would need to figure out a way to fix this problem fast.

So for the next few minutes he listened to the head buffoon apologize again and again. His fists were clenched and he felt his heart start to palpitate. The last thing he needed was a heart attack or stroke, so as the lead buffoon continued to babble, Dr. Anglim hung up the phone without as much as a sigh or goodbye. The money he was going to wire transfer in just short of the hour would stay exactly where it was. He wasn't happy about this. Money didn't mean a thing to him, it was all about the power as far as he was concerned.

9

Maya had let go of Peter's hand, "We've been walking for hours. I'm exhausted and hungry." Peter stopped walking, and turned around to face the others before explaining, "I remember a small church somewhere in this vicinity as a kid. Pop would drive up this way to take us to that lake where the fishing was excellent. Don't you remember Pop?"

Nicholas and Rita followed the three younger ones trying to keep pace, "At this point my mind is shot. Thank God your mom had the smarts to pack some bottles of water and breakfast bars in our haste to get out of the house. At least that will keep us going for a while. Just gotta ration what we have."

Pietro tried to keep his voice from sounding edgy, "Pop you gotta try to help us figure out if we're even heading in the right direction. Ditching the car was our only option. I'm sure they already found the car we abandoned. We had no choice but to walk. If we could just put our minds together and figure where that old church is, we can hole up in there until we come up with a plan. It's our safest bet right now."

Tommy started to laugh out loud, "Safest bet? Really Pete! I feel like we are walking in circles and all you got for us is the safest bet. How about we face the facts. Whatever you got yourself into now got us into it as well. Enough so that we are being hunted down, and if they don't kill us it's only a matter of time until we will drop dead on a certain day. From what, you yourself aren't even sure of. I thought you were included in all top secret strategies. I guess they failed to include you in one major fact. What it is that caused all ninety-nine and hundred year olds to die on their given age day, and from what Pete? Give us a break already!"

Pete had heard enough, "Fuck you Tommy! I didn't ask for any of this. That's why I'm here right now. What I have in my backpack can save all of mankind. We just have to get it in the hands of the right people."

"And how do you suppose we do that brother? Here in the middle of nowhere? No car, no church in sight and barely enough water and bars to sustain us for a day or two. But YOU big brother, you are the savior. So SAVE us."

Tommy rushed head down straight for his brother's stomach. If Peter was off even a beat, his brother would have knocked the wind out of him. Having missed his intended target, he spun around and threw himself on top of Peter knocking him to the ground. Fists were flying but not really making any connections.

Maya was first to try to step in and break it up, "Stop it! Just stop it!"

Rita and Nicholas pushed past Maya and Rita yelled, "Stop this right now! Get off of your brother immediately Tommy! Do I make myself clear?"

They continued wrestling and flipping one another over in the dirt. They were zoned out to what both women were saying. It wasn't until Nicholas reached down and grabbed both of his son's by their shirts that they looked up to see who had such a strong grip on them.

"Cut this shit out right now! I'll give you both five seconds to let go of each other before I jump in and trust me it won't be a pretty picture. Do I make myself loud and clear? This is NOT the time for this bullshit."

Peter pushed off of Tommy and stood up as Tommy let go of his grip on him. Tommy stood up next and brushed himself off just as Pete finished doing the same.

"Now apologize to Pietro! And I mean make it a true apology. We have enough tension without you two adding any unnecessary BS to it. You heard me. Apologize."

Tommy walked up to his brother and extended his hand in a gesture of shaking it. Peter in return put his hand out and they both shook hands.

"Sorry bro. I just lost it. This is all too much for me. I guess I'm scared and took it all out on you. If you didn't do what you did, none of this would matter in the long run."

"It's all cool Tommy. If it were the other way around I probably would have reacted the same way. We just have to stay calm and work together. I mean look at us all. I'm sure we're all scared half to death. But at least we're together for now. Hopefully God will be on our side and we'll get to where we need to."

Maya, who once again held hands with Peter, was the last to speak before they continued on their way in search of the rundown church deep in the woods. "Scared is putting it mildly. More like scared shitless to say the least."

10

"Ssh, lower your voice Myleka. They may hear you."
Myleka walked over to her thirty eight year old mother and apologized for speaking a bit too loud. Laureen gently stroked her daughter's head as she continued to watch the group of five walk through the woods. "These people must be what this craziness these past few days is all about. A sorry looking bunch if you ask me. I guess with all they've been through from what we witnessed from atop this hill would make anyone batty."

Laureen looked over at Bill and with her voice at the same lower volume as his continued, "Seems to me they are heading in the direction of our shelter. What happens if they stumble upon the closed up church where we're holding up?"

"Guess we cross that bridge when we get to it. Ain't nothing we can do unless we jump off these rocks and confront them." Bill looked over at the four faces he had spent the last few weeks with. Not one of them looked ready to meet these strangers. Having all been from the surrounding towns, each one of them conscientiously made a decision to flee their environments. Without being vaccinated, the pressure was heavily put upon them to get a shot. Threats of imprisonment and what they could expect if they didn't get the vaccination made them run like bats out of hell. Bill Whitman was a local handyman, never married, no kids and forty three years old. He was a confirmed bachelor and liked his lifestyle. He first came across Laureen and Myleka Banks as he parked his van off Route 28 and walked the 3 miles in the forest until he came upon the old run down boarded up church. In these parts of the woods there was no racial tension, so when he first stumbled upon Laureen and her eleven year old daughter Myleka, he was more surprised to see two African American women alone in the woods. Approaching them with caution, it didn't take long for them to share their stories and reasons for why they were there and where they were headed. Bill did indeed stock his van with supplies, enough to last him a few months provided he rationed accordingly. Now with three mouths to feed, he would really need portion control.

Laureen barely had time to get her and her daughter safely from their home as two white vans with the Epigen Hyperspace logo were parked on the block. Laureen watched as two groups of medical experts in what appeared to look like a uniform from an alien movie, were knocking on certain neighbors' doors.

Having been a close knit block, Laureen knew which of her neighbors hadn't been vaccinated. Surmising that as the reason for their visit, she quickly filled two backpacks with basic essentials to get them to the safety of the old run down church. Knowing it would take close to twenty or so hours on foot to reach the abandoned building, she grabbed a dozen or so water bottles and whatever food she could fit in an environmentally safe grocery bag. Sneaking out the back of her house and jumping over the backyard neighbor's fence, she was able to make her getaway before they discovered she went missing. Working on the overnight shift as a CSA (Clerical Service Associate) at the local hospital, in just a few short hours they would be alerted as to her disappearance. After an hour walk to Main Street, Laureen was able to hail a cab to take her to the outskirts of her town, where from there, their twenty plus hours trek awaited.

Upon almost walking straight into one another deep in the woods, Laureen was fast to size up Bill.

Laureen was almost as tall as the average man, standing close to six feet. Her daughter's genes were more of her ex-husband's, and she barely reached five feet. Laureen was hoping this would change once she had her first growth spurt. They both were more on the lean side with dark hair and darker brown eyes.

Bill, on the other hand, looked like he came straight off the boat from Ireland. With a strapping frame and his reddish blonde hair, he resembled a lighter version of Paul Bunyan.

A friendship formed fast and within the first week it was like they had never been strangers. Being the handyman he was, Bill was able to get into the boarded up church without much effort. Together, they cleaned it up the best they could with the supplies Bill had stocked in his van. What had once been a left to ruin abandoned church, now resembled somewhat of a home away from home. They left most of the windows boarded up except for planks taken from a window covering every direction of the church. Bill wanted to be able to see in the directions of East, West, North and South. Most of the pews were either sold or given to parishioners long ago, and there were only about four or five left. The altar had been cleared as well with just a large cross of Jesus that still hung in the center of the main altar. Hanging almost twenty feet off the ground, it remained either due to its height, or it was left to sanctify the purity of the establishment.

It was about ten days into their stay at the church when Bill decided to do a food run, hoping to also come across a cabin that he could scavenge. He felt it would be more beneficial to get more supplies just in case a winter blizzard kept them holed up for longer than anticipated. Bill took the van from its hiding spot covered by brush and drove where he knew some winter homes were only used during ski season. With not much snow for this time of year, he was hoping some were still left locked up for the season. The gas tank was still close to full and he also had two five gallon cans stored in the church for an emergency should he need more petroleum.

Bill came across a cabin that looked as if it was vacant. Having again hid the van where it would most certainly not be spotted, he set off on foot. As he got closer to the cabin he noticed that one of the side windows had been busted out. Tiptoeing to get a better look inside, he raised himself up on his toes. Bill heard rustling from behind him and he slowly turned himself around. Not even four feet away stood two Chinese teenagers. The girl appeared to be a bit older than the boy and there was a strong resemblance making him believe they could be brother and sister. They each held a large stick that looked like a spear with a sharp edge pointed directly at him. With raised hands, he introduced himself. The two teenagers just stood there undecided as to what to do next. In a soothing voice, he tried to show that he was harmless, even though he looked like the paper towel bounty man with red-blonde hair.

"I'm Bill. I'm staying at an old abandoned church not too far from here and I was out looking for more supplies I could bring back with me. I come in no harm. I'm staying with a mother and daughter that I met out in these woods here too. Ain't here to hurt no one. If you would do me a favor and just point those spears more toward the ground, I would feel a whole lot better."

Bill noticed how the younger brother's eyes first met his sister's. It wasn't until after she pointed hers down that he did the exact same.

"I'm Linh and this is my brother Khang. Our last name is Masako but we hardly remember our parents. They were killed in a car accident when we were just seven and nine. We've been doing a good job of getting by, by ourselves." Being they were the first to emigrate here from China and the authorities were not able to contact the next of kin, they became custody of the state. Having no ability to reach a family member of any sort, child services put them into an orphanage. Since they were no longer desirable babies or of American heritage, they left them in the care of the nuns of the orphanage. Linh was six months short of her eighteenth birthday and Khang was fifteen. Linh was recently informed that once she reached her eighteenth birthday she would have to leave the orphanage without being able to take Khang along with her. This was not an option. As soon as she was told her brother would be staying behind, she devised her plan of action. Long before the vaccination had been a mandatory administration, she and her brother were gone. They snuck away in the middle of the night and have been runaways ever since. At first, the local authorities sent flyers to the close by precincts in hopes of tracking them down. Once the Rapid X virus took full effect, they were since forgotten. Surviving on pure luck and whatever and wherever they could find shelter, was all they both needed. All they wanted was to remain together, and from what Bill could tell, they seemed to be barely getting by. They were both rail thin almost to the point of malnutrition, and the brother stood about six inches taller than his older sister. Their clothes needed washing and from the looks of their appearances they both could use a hot bath.

Bill felt sorry for them and before he had even given it any thought asked, "You could come back with me. We're staying at a church. We fixed it up the best we could and we have extra room if you're interested?"

"Why should we trust you? How do we know you won't turn us in?" Linh stood still defensively waiting for his reply.

"First off, have you had the chance to look in a mirror? From the likes of it I would guess you are barely eating. You more than likely have been in numerous houses in this area where food is scarce. I'm not even sure I can take on two more mouths to feed but I'm willing to bring you on board if you're game. On any given day a blizzard or Nor'easter could blow into this area and you'd be trapped with no food for what could be days. How about it? Are you willing to trust an old geezer or eventually freeze to death in these woods?"

Khang again looked into his sister's eyes for approval, but instead of letting her answer, he quickly responded, "Please sir, please lead the way. We have no other choice but to trust you. I just want you to promise to make sure we never get separated." With tears now forming in his eyes, he wiped them with the back of his sweatshirt sleeve and said, "After all, she's all I got."

11

Bill watched as the four others started to stir from their sitting positions. Laureen spoke first, "I say we confront them and see what exactly is going on. The transistor radio we have could be giving us false communications for all we know. I'd rather hear it straight from someone's mouth. Harder to lie to a person when you're face to face."

Nodding their heads in unison, both Linh and Khang also agreed with perhaps a much needed reality check.

Khang, holding his spear as if he were a warrior, confirmed what they all were thinking, "What's the worst that could happen? We have two spears and Bill you have a loaded pistol. From our vantage point, they seemed to be weaponless. If they get out of line, I guarantee we can overtake them."

"Easy there ace! Let's first meet them and see where this goes. No need for bloodshed if we can help it. Let's surround them up ahead and not take them by too much of a surprise. I'd say we have about ten minutes before we cross paths. Plenty of time to not make any rash decisions. Let's stick together and head them off at the path."

12

Peter was beginning to lose hope. It was getting close to dusk and in another hour or so the sun would be setting. With the darkness there would be dropping temperatures too. Although they were all in winter garments, if the temperature dropped below freezing, frostbite would surely set in. As it was his parents were lagging behind, more so than just a few hours prior. Tommy and Maya hadn't said much in the past hour and the conversation was minimal. Before it got too dark and it was pitch black, they would need some sort of shelter for the night. Just where and what type of protection was racking his brain.

Bill and the others waited patiently. He saw them in the distance and timed it so that they would be crossing paths within the next two minutes. They took position by the largest tree in the direct line of the path. Laureen and Myleka on one side of it while Linh and Khang stood on the other. Bill placed himself smack in front of it so he would be the first one the group would notice. If they did have any hidden gun, he would sacrifice his life first in order to protect this group he now considered his family.

Maya took notice of Bill first. She tugged on Peter's hand holding him back from going any further. Peter, in his haste to find any sort of shelter, didn't even notice the strapping man just a few yards away. There was still a bit of daylight left but the shadows made it more difficult to see too far in front of you. Tommy was second to see the group of people waiting by an enormous tree. Coming up from behind were Nicholas and Rita who both at the same time also saw the others.

Tommy shouted to his brother to forewarn him before he got any closer, "Pete, stop! Look straight ahead. They seem to be holding some sort of weapon. Bro, proceed with caution. Looks like only one big guy but who knows if others are lurking in these woods."

Peter let go of Maya's hand and told her to stay back with his parents. He then instructed Tommy to join him by his side as they walked closer to what he didn't know were friends or foes.

Bill watched as the other group of five first spotted them. The girl seemed to be holding the guy who led the group back. Another younger guy came to stand alongside the other guy. A slightly older couple stayed furthest back from the others. Bill contemplated the best way to acknowledge them. After giving it fast consideration he proceeded with, "Howdy folks. What brings you out here in this neck of the woods at this hour of the day?"

Peter put his arm out straight to stop his brother from proceeding. "We could be asking you the same thing. You're out in the middle of nowhere as well? What's your deal?"

Bill knew if he didn't nip this in the bud and fast, they would be going back and forth with tit-for-tat all night. "Ain't gonna lie, we've been watching you folks kinda all day. We heard an explosion early this morning, came out of our hiding to investigate and shortly thereafter we saw you bunch here in these woods. Care to explain what in God's name is going on?"

Peter looked at his brother and then back at his group that were now getting colder by the minute. "Too long of an explanation to go into out here in this forest. We come in peace. Can't say others out here are peaceful from what we've experienced so far. Had no choice but to ditch our car and try to find some shelter where we could lay low for a few days before deciding what we needed to do next. You seem like decent people or you would have used those weapons on us by now."

Peter stared at this unlikely bunch of people. A white man, two black girls who looked like a mother and daughter, and two Chinese teenagers, couldn't get more diverse than this. Peter didn't feel the need to beat around the bush. What he needed now was to get his family out of the cold and somewhere safe, even if for a short while. With pleading in his voice he asked, "Actually, we really could use a place to warm up before nightfall. Any assistance in this matter would be greatly appreciated. Don't know how much longer we can go on without a place to sleep tonight."

Bill had heard enough. He was a good judge of character and from the looks of this group, they appeared to be decent people. "To be honest, we have noticed strangers in these parts the last few days. We know our way around so we were able to spy on them without them taking notice. I had a sense they were up to no good and this morning when we heard that blast, it confirmed what I had been thinking all along. If what they blew up was intended for you, it would be unfair of me as a Christian man not to do the right thing. Line up your bunch and follow us. We're staying at an old abandoned church not too far from here."

Peter looked back at his girlfriend and then his parents as if to say how ironic that the place they were in search of, was where this other group had been staying. Now as they followed the man who appeared to be their leader deeper into the woods, Peter counted his lucky stars that they were lucky enough to have ran into this other group of hopeful people.

13

The wind had picked up just as they arrived at the church. The ten people, half of whom were strangers to Pete and his family, led the way up the old wooden steps to enter the church. Bill opened the door and ushered the others in. A crack of thunder shortly followed and a downpour soon after. Tommy was the last to enter and in the brief moment before he did, he was drenched by the torrential downpour.

"Quick, get in and close the door! Khang, go throw some logs in the stove up on the altar. Laureen, help him get it started while I get the others settled in. Who knows how long this storm will last or just how bad it will get."

Peter noticed how the others listened to him bark out orders without any resistance. He knew the four depended on him as he was the only adult male in the group.

"I guess introductions are in order. My name here is Bill, the woman helping with the fire is Laureen and her daughter Myleka. That over there getting the firewood is

Khang and over at the front of the church is his sister Linh. Been here a little over five weeks. Found me this wood burning stove just in the nick of time at one of the vacant cabins not too far from here. Gonna need it with the cold fast approaching."

Looking up as the rain pounded the roof of the church, Bill continued "Now look at it here. Pouring so hard this darn roof has more holes in it than a pin cushion. Linh, why don't you and Myleka grab a couple of pots and see about collecting those drips from the ceiling. I'm just about ready to hear exactly who these people are and what the heck their deal is."

Peter was the first to speak and for the next twenty minutes introduced each family member and what had exactly taken place from when he first fled the laboratory of Epigen to their run in with this group just moments ago. As he was finishing up, a branch from a nearby tree smacked up against one of the larger stained glass windows causing most of the group to jump half out of their skins.

Nicholas, after regaining his composure, was the first to speak up. "Gotta tell you Bill. I was getting worried we would freeze to death out there. God answered our prayers by having you all save us. Can't thank you enough. Just don't know how we are going to get what my son has planned and accomplished as fast as we can. Seems to me that our days are numbered and we best act fast."

"Pop, like I said time and time again, if we don't get this vial I have in my backpack to the President of the United States, within the next thirty days, either way we are doomed. Dr. Anglim will stop at nothing until only he and his selective group are all that are left. We don't have much time. We have to get to the Capitol and we have to get there fast. There is no other plan; we have no choice and we don't have much time either."

For the next hour as the rain pelted the old church like bullets riddling a wall, the ten sat gathered around the wood burning stove sharing some hot soup and crackers while bouncing methods of strategy off one another. Myleka, Maya and Khang were the first to excuse themselves to get some shuteye. The others would remain sitting in a circle as they added more logs to the fire, all the while discussing ideas on how to get to the President safely without getting killed in the process. Bill and Laureen had decided it best to join efforts with this group to ensure the safety of millions of innocent lives. Having not been vaccinated, they were being hunted as well and were the most in jeopardy of being terminated on their age related death day according to what Peter had explained. Unlike Bill and Laureen, the rest of his group were the best gamble on going the longest with no threat of extinction. Contemplating all the pros and cons of which path to take, a vote was taken and a decision was made. It was best to leave the tranquility of the rundown leaky church sooner than anticipated, so it was determined that on the third day from this evening, they too would rise up and save humanity.

14

That night as the ten had dozed off one by one, they all had completely forgotten that a new year just rang in. Each and every one of them was frazzled in their own ways and lost track of the exact end of one year and the start of another. They were all consumed with getting to Washington D.C. the fastest way possible. Realizing that the first two days of January sacrificed the lives of all centenarians and ninety nine year olds confirmed Peter's calculations. Time was of the essence and the sooner they acted on their plan, the sooner they would stop the insanity of one mad man.

15

Myleka was crying and trying to speak at the same time, "Mommy, mommy come listen!" She was the first to wake them on the third morning of their planned departure. One by one the others started to stir as they heard sobbing from the front of the church. The storm, which lasted two full days, had since passed over and bright sunshine shone in the stained glass windows high above the floor where they slept.

Laureen unzipped herself from her sleeping bag and quickly jumped to her feet. Hearing her daughter's pleas startled her from a deep sleep and she was fast on her feet. "Myleka sweetheart. What's the matter? You're scaring mommy. Take a deep breath baby. What has you so frightened?"

As the others all sat up and were stretching or yawning to the start of a new day, Myleka grabbed the small transistor radio and turned up the volume. Tuned to an AM station somewhere along the east coast, they all listened as the broadcaster continued with his shocking morning details. It seemed that all people from ninety six to ninety eight had perished the day before. It was January 4th and only the fourth day of the New Year. According to what Dr. Anglim had devised, he was stepping up his game faster than originally planned. It was to be one age group per day, not the three linked together in a bracket. At this rate there was no telling the lunacy the evil Doctor had in mind. It seemed that each day at precisely twelve noon on Eastern Standard Time the demise of an age group would take place.

Tommy pushed himself out of his sleeping bag and jumped to his feet, "Scary to say but in five short hours another group of unwilling individuals will meet the same fate. Whether they want to or not, they'll have no choice. We need to get our asses up and outta here and we need to do it right now."

Rita had just lowered her arms from stretching and reprimanded her son, "Between you and Pietro, I honestly don't know who has a worse gutter mouth. You certainly don't take after your father or me."

Maya, having been treated like a daughter herself, couldn't resist and had to put her two cents in, "Honestly mom, with all the shit and excuse my language that's going on, cursing should be the least of our worries."

Now, as the ten listened to the broadcaster as they sipped morning coffee or drank some milk along with the eggs and sausage Laureen had prepared, total devastation had claimed the world. Civilization that the world once knew, no longer existed. Societies were collapsing and no one knew exactly why or what was causing these bizarre occurrences or how to stop them.

Pete held his cup of coffee and stared at the others around him. He knew that they were the only chance to stop the madness and prevent the ultimate destruction of mankind. He had to get the vial which held the antidote into the right hands. Time was running out, and they were still hundreds of miles away from their destination. Pete silently prayed it wouldn't be their final destination.

16

"Dr. Anglim, please hold on for the President." Dr. Anglim knew exactly what President Neubert would be inquiring about. He had his answers already prepared for the questions beforehand. All he needed to do was sound convincing and all would be okay. In the last few days, the general population across the world from ninety six to hundred years old had succumbed to an untimely death. The molecules that took the doctor three years to master had proven not only successful but highly controlled in any environment. Basically what that meant was that no one could escape the aftermath once the injection was administered. Aside from antigens, ingredient components of a vaccine include adjuvants, added to enhance the immune system response, antibiotics, to prevent contamination during the manufacturing process, and preservatives and stabilizers. The vaccine worked by training the immune system to recognize and combat pathogens, either viruses or bacteria. Dr. Walter Anglim added such a small liquid adjuvant that caused a cerebral hemorrhage, better known as a hemorrhagic stroke. Mastering this effect took many experimental tries on unwilling animals of a variety of species. Starting with rodents, then larger animals such as cats and dogs, to the eventual closest species to man, the monkey, validated the total experiment. With Peter Palumbo working closely by his side, unknowingly thinking this was to find a cure for the hemorrhage, was gratifying to the mad doctor from the start. Never in his wildest dreams did he think Peter was intelligent enough to figure out his scheme. Having given his young protégé complete access to all levels of security within the organization backfired. Knowing that Peter confiscated a vial of the antidote infuriated him. If his young protégé was able to get this in the right hands, all his hard work would have been for nothing. The doctor needed to step up his game. Instead of eliminating one age per day, he took out three years in one. By starting with the elderly and working his way down the age groups, eventually only the very young would be left and without older people to feed and protect them, they too, would diminish. Without an exact location as to where his once protégé now nemesis hid, made each day more vulnerable to the outcome of his life-long plan. Dr. Anglim had his teeth clenched and was in deep thought when a very familiar voice greeted him with a friendly hello. As he unclenched his one fist and snapped out of his trance he began the conversation with, "Yes Mr. President, how is it that I may help you?"

President Neubert was in his third year of his second term of presidency. At sixty-eight, his likeability factor was eighty four percent with the American people. Usually, whatever he promised he fulfilled and this made all the difference with his supporters. He was known to be the second tallest president right below Abraham Lincoln, standing tall at six foot three, a mere inch shorter than Abe. With a full head of white hair and a slight pouch to his belly, it almost gave him a close resemblance to jolly old Saint Nick. Now however, President Neubert was anything but jolly. The sole survival of the American citizen was out of his control. For the past few days, the elderly were dropping dead all over the United States. At the exact same time each day, a brain aneurysm struck. Regardless of each individual's health, whether excellent or poor, didn't matter. Now, the whole country was expecting him to have the answer or better yet a remedy and cure to stop the daily onslaught. Rumors were circulating that an ambush was in the making toward the White House. People wanted results, and they wanted them fast. Satisfied with the hour-long conversation President Neubert had earlier this morning with Dr. Anglim, his speech writers were busy at work. Dr.

Anglim worked closely these last few months with the CDC to create a vaccine to prevent the unaccountable deaths from the Rapid X virus that took over the entire world at an accelerated speed unimaginable. Having answered all of his concerns and questions, the President was almost ready to address the nation. Scheduled to interrupt all programming right after the rush hour commute home, his hands shook like never before. In less than twenty minutes the clock would strike noon on the east coast. President Neubert considered himself a very spiritual man, and he believed his faith got him to where he was today. Now as he sipped from the snifter of his most calming scotch, his jittery hands shook. He placed the neat Blue Label down on his solid oak desk. Taking a deep breath, he put his hands together and silently said a prayer for the safety of all mankind.

Gently pressing the red end call button on his cell, Walter Anglim knew he had averted a near mess. President Neubert believed every single lie fed to him. Plain bullshit to be truthful. President Neubert would then relay all pertinent information to his Vice President and precede in order of the chain of command as far down to the Secretary of Defense. Convincing his cabinet would be a simple task as the President was highly liked by his inner staff too. Knowing the Commander in Chief would have taken care of this issue by now would allow the doctor to continue his extinction to all but the select few. As of midnight this past night, Walter had also lied to the other world leaders involved in his termination of the civilization plan. He had hoped not to stoop so low in keeping the sanity and balance but there was no other way around the impending complications that had arisen. Dr. Anglim had ensured each world country leader involved that he would continue to monitor the situation at hand. A little white lie never hurts anyone, but in this case it might just kill you.

~

With broken English, the President of Italy Christopher Zappia was the only one uncertain as to what he was hearing. "So a this young lab employee or asa you say, smarter than most colleagues disappears and has all oura top secret credentials thata could expose us all. And we shoulda believea you why? Nonea this is a makin sense. I will not jeopardize all that I a worked so hard for. Youa told or made us all a promise to the success of this masterplan. Now we have a fugitive on our hands. Catch him or I'lla personally fly over my top bodyguards to finish this fora you."

Dr. Anglim, knew Chris Zappia the longest out of all the dignitaries. Walter truly believed Chris suffered severely from the Napolean Complex. The Napolean Complex is a theorized inferiority complex normally attributed to people of short stature. It is characterized by overly-aggressive or domineering social behavior, and carries the implication that such behavior is compensatory for the subject's physical or social shortcomings. He was a short man, barely five foot two with a stocky build and a full head of dark hair, but his presence in a room was larger than life. Dr. Anglim had already surmised that out of all his allies in this project, Christopher Zappia was the smartest of the bunch. Perhaps too smart for his own good. If the dictator of his Italian heritage couldn't be persuaded like the others, then an initial dose of his guaranteed lifeline would be eliminated without him ever being aware of what had happened. As the Italian President babbled on with his asinine requests and occasional demands, the only thoughts circulating in the mad doctor's mind were Peter Palumbo and how he needed to be immediately terminated. His only major concern, causing him a severe migraine, was how in the hell was he going to find him.

17

Throughout the world every single senior citizen awaited their fate. It was determined at this point that every day at the same time a certain age would be exterminated. Headlines on almost every major newspaper called it "Death Day" and there unfortunately was no escaping it. Hospitals, police precincts and all government agencies were flooded with older people begging for their lives to be spared. Barricades were set up blocking entrances to hospitals and urgent cares to allow the saving of lives that weren't nearly close to the ages to be killed off. Traffic jams were on almost every thoroughfare with children trying to reach their elderly parents before it was too late. Road rage was around every corner and gun control no longer was restricted. Lives were lost in meaningless crossfire as accidents involving cars, buses, trucks and any other drivable means caused unnecessary delays. Many households with elderly parents held their hands to comfort them with the general consensus that nothing could be done to stop their inevitable demise.

Elderly people wept, cried, and sobbed uncontrollably in their loved ones' arms as the minutes ticked closer to extinction time. Grandparents that could say their farewells in person did just that, while ones less fortunate chose Facetime to say goodbye. In certain countries stadiums were being used to house the old to make cleanup all the more easier when they met their demise. Stricter countries resorted to herding and forcing the elderly out of their homes and into common shelters without their consent. Nursing homes were flooded and law enforcement, as well as the National Guard, were put in place to keep families from overrunning the facilities. Depression was global all around the world. The suicide rate, along with a majority of the elderly, had quadrupled when the Rapid X virus claimed the lives of so many people. Loved ones left behind weren't coping with the loss of their loved ones and felt it was an easier option to commit the act rather than wait for a certain "Death Day" to take place. Older couples married for decades chose to take pills to overdose, while lying next to one another in bed, ensuring their passing into the afterlife took place together. Madness ensued throughout the world. Societies crumbled and nations collapsed. The economic structure of every monetary value was dissolving rapidly. In the aftermath of this catastrophe, normalcy would be a thing of the past, and as the clock struck noon, millions upon millions of more innocent lives took their last breaths and tumbled over dead.

18

Maya reached over the passenger seat of the white van that was being driven by Bill Whitmore and grabbed onto Peter's shoulder, "Please not again. Please tell me this isn't happening? Oh my God! All these poor, poor people. Why? How? When will it stop? Is this going to happen to us too?"

Hearing the quiver in her voice and the shiver of her hand on his shoulder, Pete turned in his seat so he was half facing her. Looking at the sadness and what appeared to be total defeat in all eight other pairs of eyes, he tried his best to reassure the group. "We need to stay calm and focus on the matter at hand. Normally this drive to the Capitol takes close to six hours but with all the traffic and obstacles on I-95 South, there's no telling what we might come up against. I wish I had all the answers, but I don't. All I know is we need to get this vial to the President and hopefully we can stop this madness before it's too late. I thought I knew my mentor but apparently he had other ideas that he didn't feel the need to include me in on."

"Well, that really sucks bro. The world is dying more and more each day and all you can say is how you weren't included in the master plan. Shame on you, no better still shame on Dr. Anglim and his grand scheme. I don't give a rat's ass of his determination and willingness to wipe out civilization. I want to get the chance to face him one on one and we'll see who finishes on top. I would wring that bastards…"

Tommy's voice was drowned out as a helicopter flew overhead closer than usual to the road. Upon witnessing the helicopter most cars that were traveling at a decent speed slowed down to see what the commotion might be about. Upon doing this, a sudden jam of the brakes from the cars in front of the van caused all the cars to come to a complete standstill. Bill stomped his foot just in time as the car behind swerved as they hit their brakes just as fast. A domino effect of one car hitting the bumper of the car in front of them started a chain reaction. Crunching metal to metal was heard as some of the cars were unable to slow down in time and plowed into the vehicle in front. Rita pushed closer on the floor of the van next to Nicholas. There were just the two bucket seats up front and the bench behind that which seated Maya, Tommy and Laureen. Linh, Khang, and Myleka along with Pietro's parents sat across from one another in the cargo space. Stuffed among the six were supplies and the basic necessities to ensure their survival. Nicholas put his arm around Rita's shoulder and nestled closer to her as well. The helicopter flew past the onslaught of vehicles and the whirl of the blades softened. A sigh of relief could be felt among the group. Bill was sandwiched in between a Ford Escalade and a Toyota Prius. Shortly after an orchestra of beeping horns blared. Bill put the van in reverse and slowly inched backwards. There appeared to be not much wiggle room.

Bill looked in his rearview mirror and asked, "Nick, do me a favor and look out the rear door window and yell up front when I should stop backing up. Something tells me that the helicopter is looking for something or someone."

Little did the group realize that Bill's white van had been spotted a few short days ago at the church where they sought shelter. It was while they were in pursuit of Peter that they stumbled upon the van and put a tracking device underneath the frame. Doctor Anglim instructed his team to do this with the assumption that these people were unvaccinated. As it turned out he hit the lottery as the whole bunch of them were now all together.

Nick stood up and leaned toward the window to see how much space was still available. As he was about to shout to Bill that he had another foot or so, the helicopter could be heard fast approaching again from the opposite direction. Bill took immediate action as his gut instinct to an unknown danger was near. With no guidance, he stepped on the gas and the van jerked backwards until it collided with the Ford Escape. Nick was thrown off balance but he quickly sat down next to Rita. She hugged him and put her head in his chest. The agitated driver in the Escape put down his window and was yelling obscenities with his middle finger pointed at the van. No sooner had he opened the driver's door, most likely to cause havoc, the now damaged rear bumper of the van maneuvered out of the line of traffic. Tommy patted the driver's front seat whooping along, "Now we're talking. Let's get this bad boy out of here before that whirlybird lands on top of us."

Bill pressed down on the accelerator as the van careened off the road and up on the shoulder of the Interstate. "Hold on, this might get a bit bumpy but I got a feeling things are about to get a lot worse." They had already traveled through New York and were on the New Jersey Turnpike having just passed the exits to Atlantic City. Heading to exit 2 for Swedesboro at a rate of 65mph, the van was whizzing past all the stalled traffic. Passengers in other vehicles stared in astonishment as they witnessed a fast moving van being chased down by a helicopter. The pilot of the helicopter along with his co-pilot were doing what was instructed of them. The helicopter was told to stop the van at any cost even if it meant casualties might occur. With a combined total of thirty-five years of flight experience between the two pilots, the craft hovered directly above the van. With little to no effort the pilot positioned the skids to land on top of the fast moving van to cause it to reduce the speed or stop it. Upon impact of the skids on the van, screams almost drowned out the noise of the copter. Myleka jumped up and tried to reach for her mother. The sudden impact jostled the van and she cried out, "Momma, momma! I'm scared." With an outstretched hand she lunged for her mother. Laureen unfastened her seatbelt and turned around on the bench and knelt facing the group in the back. "Sweetie, sit down! You're gonna get…"

The van lurched to the left as Bill took the off ramp on exit 2 faster than it could handle. The two right tires airlifted and the van barely stayed upright. Fingers inches apart from one another, Laureen made a desperate reach to grasp her daughter's hand. Falling short of their hands entwining, Myleka was thrown headfirst into the steel interior wall of the van. A loud clang was heard as her skull hit metal knocking her unconscious, but not before a nasty gash tore into her forehead from the shelving that hung inside the van. Blood sprayed on Linh and Khang who were huddled together. Linh was crying hysterically as her brother shielded her eyes. Laureen was scrambling to climb over the seat as Tommy, who sat between both Maya and her, pulled her back. Nick was first to react as he crawled over to Myleka and lifted her onto his lap. Rita reached for one of the duffle bags trying to remember which one held the medical supplies. Confusion erupted inside the van as

Bill held his wits about gaining distance before the copter returned and veered them off the ramp.

"Oh God no! Not my baby! Please not my baby," she wailed. Maya had her head buried in the back of the passenger seat while Peter remained silent, quietly praying Bill could get them out of this mess.

"Someone do something. Please, PLEASE! Help my baby!"

Noticing his father reacted so swiftly, Tommy now wrapped both arms around her waist to hold her down, "Please Pop, help her. Please do something. Let her be okay."

Nick hardly ever heard Tommy sound so panicked and in all reality it frightened him to hear his son plead with him. While cradling the still body of Myleka, tears formed in his eyes blurring what he hoped to accomplish. Rita, having found the first aid kit, managed to make her way over to her husband to assist. "Sweetheart, focus. Take a deep breath and stop the bleeding. You can do this." She handed Nick the iodine which he poured directly on the open wound. Sure enough, a full stinging effect caused Myleka to briefly stir. The blood continued to seep out from the gash. Rita on all fours crawled over to the other duffle bags. Rummaging through a few, she managed to grab a white cloth towel and tossed it to Nick. "Press down firmly over the cut and hold her neck up to slow the bleeding." Nick did as he was instructed. "We gotta get her to a hospital or clinic. She needs stitches. This is bad, really..." He stopped himself as he caught sight of Laureen.

"Bill, get us to a hospital or doctor! Please. I don't want my baby girl to die."

Bill paid no attention to what was being said. His only objective was to get them safely out of the way of this birdlike creature once again gaining on them. As the right tires landed safely back on ground, Bill stepped down on the accelerator. Up ahead were toll booths. Past the toll booths was a red traffic light. Without hesitating, Bill gave the van gas and sped through the light. With no specific destination in mind, he searched from left to right for a place to shield the van from the helicopter. For the time being, the copter had circled back in an attempt to reposition itself over the van again. Time was running out. Bill was losing hope. As if a miracle occurred, up ahead was a sign for an unfamiliar park he had never heard of. He made the left from Lake Avenue onto Park Drive. He drove all the way down until he was hidden by the tense forest of the park he now entered. The sign stated he had entered Lake Narraticon. Bill let out his breath that he didn't realize he had been holding. As he exhaled, he caught glimpses of what was taking place in the back of the van through the rearview mirror. Bill knew Myleka was seriously injured and needed immediate medical attention. Finding the nearest hospital or clinic was totally out of the question. Whatever emergency care Myleka was in need of would have to be administered by the group.

Realizing that the group was limited to only four adults over the ripe age of thirty, scared him senseless. Taking Laureen out of the equation since she was the distraught mother, left him with only Nicholas and Rita. As far as medical training went for the two parents was anyone's guess. Bill had no other choice. It would either jeopardize the entire group or put his faith in God that with his healing power, Myleka could be saved.

19

"What do you mean you lost them? You're in a fucking helicopter hovering over the van and you fucking lose them. How is this even possible?" yelled Dr. Anglim into one of his many burner phones. "I need Peter brought to me ALIVE!" Do you understand ME! ALIVE!!" The pilot however, continued stuttering in explaining what had happened. Dr. Anglim was again so frustrated that he threw the burner phone and watched as it shattered against his kitchen wall. He was woken up at 3am from Louisa Sanchez from Spain wanting to know exactly what was happening with their elimination plan. Each and every country involved with Dr. Anglim was on a short fuse and with Peter Palumbo still at large, things were becoming more alarming with each passing minute. The fatalities from the vaccine were in full effect and the daily impact on the death tolls was climbing. The major concern was that a young man with a definite cure in a vial could ruin the entire foundation of the organization.

Peter needed to be found and stopped immediately. Dr. Anglim wanted more than anything to kill Peter himself but all in due time. All attempts in capturing him so far had proved to be futile. The President of the United States was breathing heavily down his neck to come up with a solution to stop the onslaught of human lives. That was the last thing Dr. Anglim was worried about. The country could hold their breath before an antidote was found that would be administered to ordinary citizens. His number one priority was that Peter needed to be taken care of. At this rate the Doctor needed to devise a way in which he could lure Peter into what his young protégé would think was a safety net. A net that would catch him but would never provide any kind of safety.

20

President Neubert stood in front of the podium in his oval office of the White House. No reporters were permitted in the room however; they were allowed to have their television news station cameramen set up to broadcast the live speech. Breaking news would interrupt every station of every channel on every television set in America. His wife sat nervously off to his side anticipating what was to come. The whole nation demanded answers and President Neubert unfortunately had none. With the CDC lacking a quick fix to this untimely virus and every other major hospital and specialist in the clinical field falling short, the United States was anything but united. Each day numerous lives were being lost at the precise time every day. At that rate of the spread, within a month it was probable that humanity would become extinct. As his makeup team finished their final touches on the President, David Neubert adjusted his tie. He felt as if the tie was strangling him so he loosened the knot. Deep down he knew this speech was useless and that basically every American citizen was on their own. This would never be stated as the whole nation would crumble. As it was, the rioting and looting was out of his control with no end in sight. Now, as his whole team waited in anticipation of what he would say, the President tilted the microphone toward himself. He cleared his throat as the lights on every camera flashed green, signaling they were going live in 5 seconds. The President's face was very somber as he began to speak what he had memorized in the past two hours. His speech writers were highly educated recent college graduates that put together a very convincing speech with hope being the main objective. President Neubert could only hope for the best but feared for the worst as he looked into the cameras and started to read from the teleprompter. "My fellow Americans of the United States. It has recently been brought to my attention that a remedy to the current situation is in the making. We must be patient. We will prevail! All in due time. As your president, I promise..." President Neubert hesitated when he said the word promise. Deep down he knew for certain that this was one promise made to be broken.

21

As the van came to a full stop, Laureen broke free of Tommy's grasp and climbed over the seat to stoop down and grab onto Myleka. "Please baby girl...Wake up for momma. Pleeease..." she pleaded with her unconscious daughter. Rita scooted over to put her arm around Laureen to try and provide some sort of comfort. Bill and Peter both opened their doors and stepped out of the van. Peter was first to open the rear cab. Maya slid open the side panel door and made her way down as Tommy quickly followed. They huddled alongside Peter as they watched Bill jump into action. Climbing into the van, he worked his way over to Nick to offer assistance. Without any words spoken, Linh and Khang edged their way past and out of the van to give them more space. Each minute was critical. Myleka's breathing was shallow and her skin coloring was off. Bill instructed Rita to help remove Laureen from the van in order to provide some more working space. He knew this was an excuse so she wouldn't be in close proximity if

Myleka would pass. As he stared down into her lifeless eyes he knew it would be only a matter of time if the bleeding didn't stop and the bump on her head enlarged. There was no way to tell if there was a brain bleed without the proper equipment to diagnose the internal injury.

As Nick and Bill provided medical care, Tommy tugged on his brother's arm, "Pete, we just can't stand here and watch. We got to do something. Anything."

Peter, looking quite perplexed, answered, "Like what bro? If the bleeding doesn't ease up, she'll bleed out and it's game over."

"Game over? Did I hear you just say game over like this is some sporting event. We're talking about a young girl's life, and you say it like she's a failed field goal attempt," Maya cried.

Peter turned to look into his girlfriend's eyes, "I'm sorry. I didn't mean to say it like that. I feel so helpless. We should spread out and search the grounds for any source of help."

Tommy laughed, "We're in a park. What kind of help can we find? Listen to yourself bro."

"Well, do you have a better idea? We can't drive off with a helicopter still searching for us. How much time do you think we have before they spot us again? We have to reach the White House and show them this vial before it's too late. At any rate, we can't do anything until we know if Myleka will pull through. I'm sorry if I'm sounding less compassionate than all of you. If what is happening every day at the stroke of twelve noon keeps happening, it will only be a matter of time for all of us. I pray Myleka makes it. I guess time will tell."

Peter looked at the rest of the group. Maya held her two hands to her face as she cried into her palms. Linh and Khang held hands and looked to be praying while Rita held tightly to a sobbing Laureen. Tommy stormed off and looked to be kicking at a tree stump to take out his anger in their current situation. A situation that looked anything but hopeful. Peter turned back to the open back door and watched as his father and Bill worked effortlessly to keep Myleka alive. With all that was happening, he prayed that they would all still be living when this was over.

22

"Oh God! What should I do? It looks bad from over here. Should I venture out and see if they need assistance? What if that person dies and I just watch? I promised myself when I took my boards that I would be the best nurse possible. Oh God help me decide" Karin spoke out loud as she spied on Peter and the others from the nearby bushes. Trying to keep her voice down, she continued talking aloud, "Relax Karin, that was over twenty years ago. You're forty-four. Way past keeping promises. Just walk over there. You have a medical bag with plenty of useful supplies. Stop debating and make your move." Karin Simmons, a registered nurse at Christiana Care Christiana Hospital in Newark Delaware, left the Emergency room in a sheer panic. Having scheduled appointments for most of the day vaccinating the younger children in the surrounding communities, Karin felt that something just wasn't right. Over the last few weeks, certain doctors of the hospital were organizing vaccinations to all families that were not available or missed the first rounds of the death induced needles. Dr. Anglim's staff had notified every hospital in the country to open up a second lethal batch to those who never received one to date. People and their families flocked to receive what they thought to be the lifesaving dose, unaware of the actual effect to be given. Still, there were some families unwilling to oblige, and they were rounded up by the National Guards and taken to the hospital. Fear and uncertainty were etched on their faces, and whether or not they wanted the injection, it was given. Karin, having been a nurse for over two decades, felt it in her gut that something was not right. All hospital employees were required to get the vaccination at the beginning of the outbreak to continue to work. Karin felt safer once she did. Now, however, her gut told her differently. Seeing how hospital policy required every individual who entered the emergency room to get the vaccination was now concerning. What had once been an individual's choice, was now a requirement. This morning totally rubbed Karin the wrong way, watching young families with toddlers and infants lining up to get their loved ones the vaccine for the Rapid X virus. The head doctors were pushing all the nurses to step up their game and get these families injected. Karin was nauseated watching this unfold. Young children and babies were crying and some had to be held down to administer the needle. When a mother or father started to object to their loud child's cries, a National Guard would be alerted and the family was given no choice but to follow along. When Karin went on her morning break, which was when she made her final decision, she excused herself from her coworkers by saying her stomach was troubling her. She needed the bathroom and she stressed just how fast she needed it. Grabbing her pocketbook and keys and making sure her cell phone was on hand, she fled the hospital via the main entrance. She didn't want to attract any unwanted attention from exiting the emergency room entrance. Quickly heading to the employee parking garage, she started her 2018 Jeep Wrangler and fled the lot. The attendant who helped assist the employees as they entered and left the parking garage jumped back as she sped out the garage. Usually, Karin would roll down her window and state a greeting whether it be good morning or good evening but today was not the case. Solely focused on getting far far away from the hospital, Karin drove her Jeep onto I-95 heading north to a destination she had given no thought to. Single, with no husband or children, she had no binds to where she would wind up. Putting as much distance as possible between the hospital and herself was her only goal right now. Having driven at a speed unsafe to her usual driving capacity, she travelled for the last thirty minutes or so in a blur. Afraid, uncertain and in somewhat of a daze, it wasn't until she was approaching exit 2 on the New Jersey turnpike that for some odd reason, her instinct told her to go to Lake Narraticon State Park. She had been there numerous times over the years, since it gave her a sense of peace and tranquility. Now as she relaxed and tried to regain her composure, panic once again tried to instill itself in her. A helicopter was flying overhead and circling the area. Then out of the blue, a van came speeding into the park going way too fast. Sensing things were about to go down, rather than drive off, Karin exited the Jeep Wrangler and ran for cover in the surrounding bushes. For a woman of forty-four she still had the figure she had as an eighteen year old. Standing at five foot seven and weighing a mere one hundred twenty, she sprinted across the parking lot before the van screeched to a stop just yards away. Within minutes the van's back doors sprung open and mass confusion took place. From what Karin could tell, someone needed urgent medical care that these people were unable to provide. Going back and forth and speaking aloud to herself, Karin had made her final decision. She scrambled out of the bushes, headed to her jeep to grab her medical bag she always kept handy for these just in case emergencies, and made her way over to the van.

23

Tommy, having returned from his temper tantrum, was the first to notice the blonde haired woman fast approaching the van. Tapping his brother on the shoulder and pointing in the direction the woman was coming, Peter yelled, "Whoa, who are you? Hold off there Miss. Where do you think you're going?" Peter quickly tried to surmise the woman dressed in hospital scrubs who came out of nowhere. Hearing Peter shout at this stranger had the remaining group members all look in her direction. Without a moment's hesitation, Karin wasted no time in introducing herself and readying herself to help. She quickly stepped up and into the back of the van. Placing her medical bag on the floor and opening it to grab what she thought might help, she accessed the current situation. Myleka was bleeding out and having placed her hand over her wrist to feel a pulse, Karin asked Bill and Nicholas to give her some space. Both men glanced at one another looking relieved that a medical professional had intervened. Working furiously, Karin broke out in a sweat. Padding, suturing and monitoring Myleka's vitals were the only objective to Karin's determination to save this young girl's life. Laureen had let go of the support Rita provided and leaned on the back door of the van silently but enough to be heard praying, "Thank you Jesus! Whoever this angel is, thank you for sending her to me for my baby girl. Please let her save my daughter's life. I put my trust in you Jesus and I ask my Lord to guide this angel along. Oh, JESUS, I thank you from all my inner soul I have to offer." With Laureen's arms now outstretched and straight up in the air, she swayed back and forth crying hallelujah.

Maya hugged Peter as she too, started to pray the 'Hail Mary'. Before she even finished the first line, Tommy and his mother, Rita, started to pray along… "the Lord is with thee. Blessed are thou…" They all chanted now as Linh, Khang and both brothers prayed as well. Continuing, they all recited… "pray for us sinners, now and at the hour of our deaths…" Nick was the first to scream out as he just caught a glimpse of Myleka straining to open her eyes, as Karin continued working feverishly on her. "Holy Mother of mercy! Her eyes just blinked and I think she is trying to open them," shouted Nick. Bill joined in, "By God, I can't believe this. The bleeding has stopped and her breathing has picked up. A true miracle if you ask me! A Goddamn miracle!"

All among the group tears flowed. Laureen jumped in the van and took hold of her daughter's hands sobbing and babbling at the same time. She patted this angel on the back and quickly noticed how drenched Karin was. For the past forty-five minutes this angel in disguise performed procedures only a licensed professional could, and from the outcome of her knowledge of medicine and her ability to work so fast, it looked very promising for her daughter Myleka. Just a short time ago, her fate appeared dismal. Now, within the past few minutes Myleka's hands were moving and she appeared to be coming around by blinking her eyes in reply to the questions Karin was asking. Myleka was going to make it. If not for Karin, this would have not seemed possible. Karin used all her skills and expertise over the years and it paid off. She was able to stabilize Myleka, stop the bleeding and stitch up the nasty gash on her forehead. Starting an IV and administering a painkiller and antibiotic would ensure the healing process in a speedier time frame. Amongst tears, cheers and wallops of joy, the whole group was celebrating the survival of one of their own. Myleka was just moments away from death and now she would live. Living was what they all hoped for, but not one of them knew exactly for how long.

24

"Okay, so let's make sure we get this straight. What is it we will exactly be gaining by warning other parents just what they are having done to their children? An instant death sentence for each and every one of them," Tommy insisted as he had the whole group's attention. It was fast approaching late afternoon and Myleka's condition immensely improved over the course of the day. Karin had shared her story of how she narrowly escaped imprisonment of her own. Bill and Peter thanked her for coming out of hiding when she did. Laureen also thanked her numerous times over the last few hours. Her daughter's life was spared by her quick acting skills. Karin informed the group of what was being done to all unvaccinated minors at the hospital where she fled. After she finished her nightmarish tale, Peter was the first to suggest, "We got to stop them! We can't let them kill these innocent children. We need to warn their parents."

"Warn them, why? In a matter of time, the parents won't be alive to care for them. Did you even stop to think about that? Every day a different age group dies. What's to say that it continues to be a countdown from one hundred to zero. That eliminates all their parents before them," Maya tried to reason with her boyfriend. Her eyes filled with tears and Rita went over to comfort her. "She's got a valid point. No use jeopardizing our safety in all likelihood that it would be pointless. We need to get to the President, Peter. You need to make him aware of what's going on and who's to blame for all this. Put a stop and hopefully administer a cure to the rest of the country while it's possible."

"I agree whole heartedly with mom on this bro. Let's get in the van and speed the fuck outta here. God knows what's waiting for us around every corner."

"Listen, I hear what you all are saying, but in light of this dismal feeling about the whole situation, I feel the best way to settle this is to vote on who wants to warn them versus the latter option and speed the fuck away," Bill mentioned to the entire group.

"Sounds fair to me," Nick answered first.

"I second that," announced Rita shortly after.

And one by one the remaining group all agreed on a fair vote.

Bill took the initiative to start the voting, "All those in favor of going to the hospital to warn the parents, raise your hand."

Being young themselves, Linh and Khang were the first two to raise their arms in agreement. Laureen followed suit and her arm was next to shoot up in the air. Bill as well put his hand up. "That makes four in favor of heading to the hospital," Bill announced. He then went on to ask the following, "All those in favor of hauling our asses out of here and to the White House, raise your hands."

Simultaneously, Nick, Rita, Tommy and Maya all put their hands up. Peter hesitated for a brief moment before he, too, decided speeding off deemed the best outcome. That made the count 5-4 in lieu of not warning the parents of the much younger children. Having just entered the group, Bill asked Karin to cast her vote as she was now a part of this newly made family. Karin looked totally decisive in how to cast her vote. She witnessed first-hand the mayhem at the hospital and feared for the fate of the group. On the other hand, innocent children were being vaccinated with a dose of a lethal injection. Guilt-ridden, she stared at the ground and speaking in a lower voice than most could hear without straining, she answered rather than raise her hand, "God forgive me, but I say let's get the hell away from here. Alerting the President of the United States will save countless lives if we get to him before it's too late."

25

Making room for another passenger was no easy task. Myleka took up quite a lot of room in the back of the van. Laureen now sat alongside of her, freeing up a spot in the second row of seats. No one spoke while Peter and Bill helped make room to accommodate eleven passengers now. The decision was made by a fair vote but tension seemed to linger in the air. No one spoke for the initial exit from the park. Whether it was from uneasy feelings to let innocent children die or the threat of impending doom cast upon the van, managed to quiet them all. Unbeknownst to them was that the last child had been vaccinated with the deadly component just moments before they took their final vote.

26

Conversation was at a bare minimum as Bill drove the van along I-95 with Peter riding shotgun. Peter was the lookout for any unusual activity whether it be by land or air. They had driven the last hour and forty five minutes with no activity to delay their destination. This seemed very odd as the helicopter attack came out of nowhere. "So where to now? Do we head straight to the White House and ask for President Neubert? You know we'll never get past the Secret Service. Our only hope is that I present my ID from Epigen Hyperspace. It has to work. I have to convince them that we must speak with the President immediately," Peter rambled to Bill who sat quietly listening while he drove.

"You can do this! I have complete faith in you to get us to the President. If anyone can, it's you," Maya reassured her boyfriend.

"Bro, do whatever it takes. There's no other choice at this point. If we don't get the word out to the President, we're even more doomed then we already are," Tommy said with a bit more enthusiasm than warranted.

"I hear the both of you. Won't be long now. Bill, follow Constitution Avenue to 15th Street and turn left. Then follow 15th Street to Pennsylvania Avenue and turn right. On the right we should see three blue awnings and above the door it should read 'The White House Visitor Center'. We should be approaching Constitution Avenue shortly."

Up ahead was Constitution Avenue. Bill slowly made the right onto the road and followed the exact directions Peter had just mentioned.

Bill was excited to see the blue awnings as he steered the van right toward the lot. Roadblocks were setup all around the entire White House with National Guard trucks surrounding each. Soldiers stood by as the van slowly made its way. There were so many other vehicles pulled over along the side of the road that the entire scene looked quite eerie. Families were in most of the cars and the soldiers were inspecting the occupants. It appeared that the drivers were asked to step out of their cars as most motorists were not behind the wheels. Bill and Peter took caution but continued on their journey. Not a single National Guard slowed their progress. They stopped the van right alongside the awnings.

Bill, who had remained quiet most of the drive, finally spoke up. "I'm not liking the feel of this. Not one bit. I say we turn around and high tail our asses outta here. Something doesn't feel right."

From the rear of the van, Nick had been watching all along from the large windows and said, "I think this is a setup. Why let us through and not stop us? High tail it is right. Something ain't Kosher here."

"Yes, PLEASE. I feel it too. I think we just drove into a trap," Rita also shouted from the back.

Sensing imminent danger now, Bill put the van in reverse. From the right side of the White House, seven Black Escalades with tinted windows sped around the corner. Bill accelerated the gas, but the Escalades surrounded the van in a complete circle preventing a clear escape path. Bill took his foot off the gas and stepped on the brake. Ramming through the posse of cars would put his passengers at risk of serious injuries. From what the group could see, at least twenty or so Secret Service Agents exited their vehicles with their guns drawn and aimed at the van. Laureen, Linh and Maya were all frantically pleading with Bill do to something. Khang, who rarely spoke, also joined in with the women as he held tight to his sister to provide comfort to her.

One of the agents who must have been in charge of the others, slowly walked over to the van with a megaphone in his hand and spoke clearly into it. "Step out of the vehicle! I repeat step out of the vehicle NOW!"

Bill frantically looked over at Peter for reassurance. "Shit, what do we do now? This is bad. Real bad. I should have sensed something as we drove here without a hitch. What the fuck do we do now?"

Knowing that an additional ten lives were hanging on a thread, Peter in what he hoped was a soothing voice said, "I say we do as they ask. If we refuse, they'll only storm the van and drag us out."

"Seriously bro? Are you fucking insane! Just open our doors and get out like we're joining these assholes at a picnic!"

"Calm down Tommy! We don't even know for sure if they're on our side or not."

"From the looks of how they have us surrounded and with their rifles drawn, it doesn't paint a pretty picture."

"I agree with your brother. Just look around. Sorry Peter, but this doesn't feel right," Maya interjected.

"Listen, I say we all get out slowly and I'll ask to speak to the person in charge. I'll explain our situation and the need to speak with President Neubert. I mean, we got this close. We can't give up now."

After a few glances from one another, the group nodded in agreement. There really was no other choice. Pete was the first to open his door and exit the van. Before doing so, he stuffed the life-saving insulin vial in his front pocket. Realizing he may need it to convince the President, he took it out of his bag as Bill navigated the van. Upon stepping out, he was immediately instructed to put his hands up in the air and over his head. With what appeared to look like a firing squad ready to fire, did anything but comfort Pete. Glancing back at the van, Pete watched as Bill stepped out next. Tommy slid the side door open and stepped out. He reached in to help Maya and Karin out. The four of them raised their arms as Pete had done only seconds before.

Five agents rushed the back of the van. The largest of the group pulled the two handles and stood back as the doors opened. The agent with the megaphone from the front Escalade barked urgent orders for the occupants in the back to quickly exit. Nick shuffled to the edge and was the first to get down from the back ledge of the van. He helped his wife Rita down next.

Khang jumped from the back startling a few of the agents that quickly raised their weapons. Sensing that wasn't the smartest approach, he leaned in and took hold of his sister's hand and helped her out. They held onto one another until they were instructed to put their hands immediately in the air. They did as they were told. One agent pushed past the four standing at the back of the van and saw that two more people remained inside. The agent with the megaphone must have been informed through his earpiece as he once again warned the two remaining to step out. Laureen, who held tightly to her daughter Myleka since awakening shouted from inside the cargo area. "Please! Let us be! My daughter is hurt and shouldn't be moved. Just LEAVE US ALONE!" Her demand fell on deaf ears. Two agents reached in and grabbed her by her arms, dragging her from the back pulling her out. Tommy, who was at the side of the van quickly sprung to action. "Didn't you fucking hear her? Her daughter is hurt! Let go of her!" He was ready to assist however possible. Before he even managed to take a few steps, three agents grabbed him by the arms and held him tightly in place. "Let go of me you pieces of shit!" He kicked his feet trying to break free. He pulled so hard that his right arm broke loose. He was swinging his fist wildly in the air but not before it connected with one of the Secret Service Agent's jaws. The agent fell to the ground clutching his chin in his hand. Two other agents rushed from a different direction and one of them quickly tasered Tommy with no warning. Tommy's entire body twitched, his eyes rolled back in his head, and he fell to the ground where his whole body convulsed. Mass confusion ensued immediately following this. Rita screamed out and dropped to the ground to cuddle her son. Nick ran head first into the agent who had just tasered his younger son, sending him flying backwards knocking the wind out of him in the process. Bill joined in and started throwing punches at any agent that got near him. Peter watched in astonishment. Agents started appearing from every which angle grabbing on to the members of the group one by one. Khang and Linh put up quite a struggle until they were also restrained. It took four agents to subdue Bill who continued to punch, kick and squirm through the rush of madmen. Maya and Karin stood frozen in their original places like mannequins. Witnessing his brother fall to the ground and his father now being apprehended by several other agents that appeared to come out of the woodwork left him with one quick decision. He needed to break free among the total chaos and he needed to do it NOW! The President needed to be warned of the very near and fast approaching doom. This may be their last effort in doing so, or in all actuality, his last attempt since his family and friends were being quickly detained. With a quick look over at Maya, who still stood motionless, he nodded as if he warranted her approval and bolted into the crowd while the mayhem continued. He dared not look back in fear that a whole slew of agents would be upon him in mere seconds. Weaving and zig zagging, Peter broke away and gained distance as he jumped over several roadblocks. Somehow he managed to get past all the agents, who were busily subduing his group, and made it to the entrance to the Visitor Center. Peter peeked through the glass of the front door. The center looked empty at present. Knowing he had never been in this part of the White House or for that matter any part, he slowly opened the door and nervously walked in. Sweating and breathing heavily from the adrenaline rush, Peter had no idea or plan as to his next action. Guilt washed over him, making him perspire even more. Leaving his family and friends to a fate unknown, he had to make the whole mission worthwhile. He had to get to President Neubert. If he didn't succeed in doing so, then everything leading up to this would prove futile. He silently prayed for the safety of the group as he quietly made his way to areas unknown. This was his ultimate quest- to find the President and tell him everything he knew. President

Neubert must first promise to call his Secret Service Agents to release his family to safety. Once this was done, then every single detail from Epigen Hyperspace and the evil Dr. Anglim would be exposed in hopes of saving the remainder of civilization, but only if the President kept to his promises. Unfortunately, some promises were made to be broken and Peter was just about to find out how.

27

As Peter navigated the halls of the White House in search of President Neubert, the Secret Service Agents were fast descending upon him. Peter lost complete track of the direction he was heading as every turn led to an even bigger and longer hallway than the last. His first flight of stairs confused his senses and he took shelter along a wall, hiding behind a curtain to gather his bearings. When he felt somewhat confident to continue his quest, he stepped out from the long velvet curtains and headed east in hopes of finding the Oval Office. Peter slowly crept from one long hallway to the next, holding his breath as he did so. Peter felt hopeless as each step forward felt like he had taken three steps back. When he was sure that he had outsmarted the agents, his confidence slowly started to return. Quickening his pace, he took larger strides down the never ending hallways. Scanning from left to right, Peter scouted the next hallway before turning into it. As he rounded a bend to move onto the next long stretch, he was tackled before he knew what hit him. Out of what felt like the woodwork, three agents were hidden and ambushed him. He fell backwards, narrowly missing his head from hitting the tiled floor by inches. A black cloth bag was shoved over his head and his hands were handcuffed behind his back. This all took place in mere seconds. Dazed and confused, he was pushed, pulled, and prodded with barely a second to gain his balance. When Peter lost his footing, he was lifted up under his armpits and moved along. Trying to stay upright had Peter completely transfixed. A series of lefts and rights and straight paths finally came to an end when they all came to an abrupt halt. What sounded like a door being opened was confirmed as he was pushed into a room. The force of the push led Peter into a stumble which couldn't be stopped. As he tumbled to the ground, Peter rolled over onto his back and tried to kneel. A Secret Service Agent walked over and lifted the black hood off. Peter gasped for fresh air after the suffocating feeling of the last few minutes. It was then that he saw what he longed for all along. President David Neubert was seated behind the oval desk that people only saw from pictures. Peter gapped in awe as his hands were freed and he was forcibly placed in a chair directly in front of the most powerful man in the country, if not the world. Without a moment to spare, Peter started his prepared speech, "President Neubert, sir. I come in hopes of stopping what will be the end of civilization.

My family and I travelled from Long Island to warn you of the continued doom. You need to stop the madman behind all this before its too late. Catch him and shut down the whole operation. Please sir, he NEEDS to be stopped."

President Neubert listened intently with his hands folded on the top of his desk. Waiting for what appeared to be a tirade by a young gentleman he had been warned would come. Vice-President Amanda Caputo was on the West Coast trying to put an end to the everyday chaos currently taking place. This left President Neubert alone with this current predicament. Sensing that a response of some sort needed to be made, the President stared at Peter as he spoke. "And just what makes you so sure of this? Who exactly are you and who is this mad doctor you seem so eager to defile? What proof or better choice of a word, evidence do you possess to make these accusations?"

"Dr. Anglim! Walter Anglim from Epigen Hyperspace! Surely you heard of him. He concocted this plan years ago! I worked for him for years. He was my mentor! Along with a hand full of other prominent world leaders, Dr. Anglim orchestrated this whole plan. He is the mastermind behind it all. Please sir, you must believe me."

"Really, and why is that? Again what evidence do you have? Barreling onto the grounds and storming in here and you say this Dr. Anglim is the madman. I need proof."

Nearing complete panic, Peter remembered what he had placed in his jean pocket right before the agents captured his family. Reaching in, he pulled out the vial. "This right here sir can saves hundreds upon hundreds of lives. I stole it from the lab the night I fled the building. You MUST believe me! Please sir. YOU HAVE TO."

President Neubert stared at the vial, unsure what to make of it.

Stepping out of the woodwork, Dr. Anglim tried to hold back his smile, knowing the vial would once again be back in his hands.

"And why should he believe the likes of you?"

The sound of that familiar voice startled Peter so much so that he jumped up from his chair. Pointing at the figure who somehow managed to sneak up behind him, Peter loudly exclaimed, "YOU! What are YOU doing here?" Peter knew he had to protect what he had stolen from the lab, so he shoved the vial into the front pocket of his jeans again.

"I should be asking you that same exact question." Dr. Anglim asked in a rather cooler voice than Peter would have expected.

President Neubert sat silently, listening as the two figures who apparently knew one another bickered back and forth. Losing his own patience now, he demanded answers. "Frankly I don't give a shit about who did what to who. Seems like double crossing and theft of goods are involved in this matter. I have a God damn nation crumpling at our feet with mass amounts of people dying every day at the same exact time. I don't need this bullshit. I WANT ANSWERS! And you Dr. Anglim promised me I would get them."

"Precisely!" Peter shouted. "Ask him how he devised such a plan to eliminate mankind. I was there. I watched him hatch it from day one. He thought I was completely in on it. Ask him!"

"Is this true? And how is it the good doctor could cause all this death?"

Peter eagerly answered, "Timing. The timing was perfect. When the Rapid X virus struck, it made it all the more easier to jumpstart his evil plan. And with the help of other world leaders and dignitaries who jumped onboard faster than anticipated, Dr. Anglim sped it up. Ask him yourself."

For the first time, President Neubert looked baffled. Not knowing who at this point to believe, he prodded further, "And just how does he cause the loss of so many innocent lives each day at precisely the same time? Explain that young man."

Without hesitation Peter continued, "He designed a chip the size of a grain of sand with all of that person's personal information that was injected into them when they were vaccinated. All of their information was at his fingertips. He has a setup of computers designed to eliminate people according to their date of birth and ages. I witnessed first-hand how he designed it. Dr. Anglim worked on it for years.

You have to believe me. I know it sounds crazy. With a hit of a button he can literally wipe out people's lives."

"That is totally impossible and too far-fetched to even comprehend. These accusations against a prominent Doctor such as Walter himself can get you thrown in jail young man. As it is, you and your family are considered fugitives at this point for fleeing the law."

"Fleeing the law? Excuse me, Mr. President but how am I and my family fugitives? If anything, I fled a corrupt laboratory that was designing a way to wipe out civilization and I'm the fugitive? My family and the rest of these people are innocent bystanders who felt justice needed to be served as well. That makes us the bad guys? How is this even possible?"

Dr. Anglim stood by listening intently to every word spoken between the President and Peter. He knew if he played his cards just right he would have President Neubert exactly where he needed him. On his side. He had to choose his words very carefully to ensure this would happen. "Peter, Peter, poor, delusional Peter. Honestly, how did you come up with this preposterous accusation? And to think I mentored you to the best of my ability and this is how you repay me, with such ludicrous allegations. How absurd. No, actually how totally ridiculous to even fathom. David, pardon me, I mean Mr. President. You must feel horrible to have to sit there and listen to this pathetic individual. I apologize for his wasting of your valuable time during such a critical crisis with our country. After all, our relationship over the years has proved us loyal to one another in many aspects. So much so that by my company vaccinating most Americans, I assured the health of our nation, as dismal as it appears right now. Why waste anymore of your valuable time."

Shaking his head in disbelief of everything he had heard, the President knew what must be done to continue to resolve this lunacy that was extinguishing America.

Without uttering a word, President Neubert made eye contact with his three agents and it was enough for them to know what to do next.

Peter, sensing that his plea was played to deaf ears, lunged to the evil doctor. He was inches away from tackling him when one of the agents, quick on his feet, blindsided him, knocking him off balance and to the floor. Giving every effort he had left, Peter cursed, screamed, and yelled every thought possible to deface the doctor. As he tried to muster what remaining strength he had left by kicking and flaying which proved fruitless, he was once again handcuffed and forcefully led out of the oval office.

Dr. Anglim held up his hand to stop them from leaving the office. Confidently, he walked over to Peter and reached into his pocket while Peter squirmed to keep the vial safely tucked in his jeans. He was throwing up his legs to fend the doctor off. One of the agents dropped to his knees to hold both of Peter's legs together to make it easier for the doctor. Once the vial was out of his pocket, Doctor Anglim waved to have them proceed. "Take him to the others and I'll instruct you where they will all be taken. The sooner we get these fugitives off the premises the better."

"You BASTARD, you evil fucking BASTARD! You did this! You created a vaccine to wipe out mankind and you're getting away with it ALL! Open your EYES, all of YOU! Before it's too late." Then he spat in the direction of Dr. Anglim while laughing hysterically knowing that it was already too late. Although the Rapid X virus was out of their control, Dr. Anglim feasted on the aftermath and his success in what was fast becoming the demise of humanity. Peter knew he was losing the battle, but he would never give up. Turning his head around one last time as he was ushered out, he needed to say what he now felt for this hated madman who he once idolized. "May you BURN IN HELL you ruthless evil bastard! You may have fooled all these people, but God knows exactly who you are and YOU WILL PAY. May God send you to the eternal flames of hell and may your soul..." Peter didn't get to finish his sentence as he was dragged out of the Oval Office just as Dr. Anglim slammed the door, drowning out his remaining words.

28

From what Peter could remember after being forcefully dragged away from the only hope he had left, dulled his senses. As he neared the white van that was driven by Bill which felt like only moments ago, there was no one from the group left. Holding back tears to look like he appeared strong willed still, his eyes scanned the surrounding areas. There was no trace of the ten people that were now his extended family. Not a single element remained of their existence. As if they vanished into thin air. The leader of the Secret Service agents, who previously had spoken into the megaphone demanding they exit the van, slowly walked over and stood next to Peter. Peter was just about to start asking him for answers to their whereabouts, but before he had the chance he was jabbed with what felt like a needle. The pain was fast and furious and within seconds Peter felt woozy. Shortly after the wooziness, Peter fainted.

29

Peter was jolted awake. The first thing he noticed was that his hands were tied tightly to some sort of netting. Moving his wrists was impossible. Opening his eyes, he realized he couldn't see as a blindfold was placed over them. His mouth was stuffed with some type of gag. Peter tried to remain calm. He was seated on the floor of something cool from the feel of it on his backside. His legs were splayed out in front of him and were not bound like his wrists. His other sense of hearing kicked in and he heard what sounded like the engine of an airplane. Loud but not as loud as the rotors from a helicopter, he listened carefully and also heard stirring not too far away from where he sat. He assumed it wasn't a commercial airliner but probably either a military plane to transport soldiers or a common aircraft carrier for overnight deliveries. He was very close to a panic attack but managed to keep it in check when he heard others nearby moving restlessly. He tried to speak through the gag but only words that sounded like grunting came from his mouth. For a full minute he proceeded to make cave-like sounds instead of actual words. Frustrated, he finally gave up.

"Pete, is that you? Please tell me it's you. Where the hell are we and what's going to happen to us?" Tommy spoke loudly enough to be heard over the engine noise.

Wondering how his brother managed to get the gag out or even if he had one to begin with, he needed to let him know that he was correct in assuming it was in fact him.

"Hmm, hmm, meeee," Pete sputtered.

Realizing it was his brother by those few words, Tommy went on. "Oh, Thank God. I didn't know what happened to you. One second you were with us all and the next you bolted like a bat out of hell. They injected us with some sort of tranquilizer and it knocked us out one by one. I gather we are being transported on some sort of plane to God only knows where. This is insane. Right out of some sort of sci-fi movie. I have been hearing others around us squirming as they must be waking up also. They were rushing to put some sort of gag in my mouth but in their haste they didn't tape it properly. I was able to shake my head back and forth enough that the little bit of tape they did put around my head came loose. Lucky for me, I guess. Is anyone else able to talk?"

There was a moment of silence until two more voices frantically spoke up. One was Khang and the other was Karin. Both of them were rambling and throwing out random questions too fast to make sense of.

"Is Linh alright? Please Linh make some sort of sound if you're near me." From a few feet away a female voice kept mumbling. "Linh, I know it's YOU! Oh thank God or Buddha for that matter."

"As they were rushing my turn to be immobilized, I was able to leave enough space between my mouth and the gag that it practically fell out on its own. We are in a shitload of trouble. Doesn't look promising for any of us. I wonder where they could be taking us. Hopefully they have us all gathered together in one area of this plane." Then in an instant, it was as if a lightbulb suddenly went off in Karin's head. She continued, "In fact, I have an idea. I'll call out each name and if you're nearby stomp your foot or feet on the floor of the plane."

Karin slowly started with the person who she thought mattered the most, considering he played an integral part in this whole fucked up situation.

"Even though I'm almost certain your grunts to your brother already confirmed it was you, I want to play it safe and double check." Karin shouted over the engine noise, "Peter?"

A loud stomping from a few feet away confirmed his presence.

"Nick?" Again, a bang from nearly a few feet nearby answered his presence.

"Rita?" There was silence. "RITA?" A slight stirring from a different area of the aircraft was heard followed by a light tapping of both feet.

"Oh God, I forgot Peter's girlfriend's name," Karin said, feeling foolish for doing so. Tommy chimed in to speed it along, "Maya, her name is Maya. Are you with us Maya?" Loud banging before he nearly finished confirmed she was among them.

"Laureen?" Karin was startled as the foot stomping was literally right next to her, but it marked Laureen's attendance with the group.

"Myleka?" Nothing. "Myleka, please do something." Still, nothing for a full minute. Suddenly, a moan was uttered from what sounded like the voice of a much younger female.

"We have to assume that's Myleka. Maybe her strength just isn't there for her to lift her feet. Linh, I'm hoping that was you mumbling to your brother before..." Feet started banging against the floorboards rapidly to alert Karin she was correct.

"Now for Phil?"

Tommy would have laughed under any other circumstance but corrected Karin instead. "You mean Bill. Bill, are you with us?"

From all the way across the plane, mumbling and feet banging at the same time made his presence known quite quickly.

Tommy sighed in relief as Karin went on. "I believe that's all of us. At least we're all together, although these restraints don't make it any easier for us. Let's just pray that whoever these people are that whisked us away, don't harm us more than they have already. We can only hope that wherever we are being taken to will come with them releasing us with all that's going on in this fucked up world. There's enough shit going down that we shouldn't even matter." In fact the only thing that mattered the most at the present time, was eliminating the enemy. The enemy that consisted of eleven people that just finished their roll call.

30

For what felt like an eternity but was only a four and a half hour long flight finally came to an end when the group was jostled upon the wheels touching ground. The aircraft screeched to a sudden stop, throwing them forward against their restraints. Frightened as to what would come next, no one fidgeted. The side cargo door was lowered and what sounded like dozens of running feet fast approached. Everything was happening so fast. Ropes were being untied and one by one each of the eleven was hustled onto their feet. Tommy, who was able to speak loudly said, "Hey, easy there you fuck heads! And watch out for the little girl. She's very fragile after a close brush with death." The soldiers heeded to what he said regarding Myleka but took no pity on the others. Rita screamed as she was lifted up quite forcefully.

"Hey asshole! That's my mom you're fucking with. Hurt her and I hurt you. Do I make myself…" Tommy didn't get to finish his sentence as one of the soldiers ribbed him in the back with his rifle, knocking him forward and almost making him lose his balance.

After regaining his footing, Tommy blasted them again. "I swear to GOD I'll rip each of you a new asshole if you harm any of us."

"Hey, ease up there champs. No need to handle us like we're criminals. In case you're unaware, we did absolutely nothing wrong." Karin made her point loud and clear.

Unfortunately falling on deaf ears, the soldiers continued to usher the group out of the aircraft and into an awaiting yellow school bus. They had placed handcuffs on each one of them after they untied their restraints. Pushing them from behind made them all the more unstable on their feet. Maya stumbled and was lifted up so forcefully that she let out a scream even through gagged mouth. Peter pushed toward the sound and was quickly taken by both arms at the elbow and dragged onto the bus and pushed into a seat. After the whole group was loaded onto the bus, the doors were closed and the bus exited the runway toward their next destination. Possibly their final destination if what Dr. Anglim had in mind took place.

31

The eleven scared passengers felt every bump the bus went over. Being blindfolded, handcuffed and unable to speak made it even the more frightening. Eventually, the bus arrived at its intended location. Each passenger had two soldiers assigned to him or her. The soldiers were instructed to not leave their assigned person's side. One by one they were led off the bus and marched single file into a bunker. This bunker was built by Dr. Anglim five years prior in anticipation of his upcoming annihilation of civilization. The bunker consisted of a large holding area almost the equivalent size of an oversized jail cell complete with prison bars. The walls were designed to be at least one to three feet thick. The top of the bunker had at least ten feet of packed dirt to protect against cave-ins, possible radiation, and any other outside issues. The concrete foundation was made to withstand water corrosion and flooding that would occur if there was ever a major hurricane in the likes of Katrina. Dr. Anglim purchased the vacant land and then paid a hefty sum to a black market company. He found a very shady company online that supplied illegal immigrants to perform the work needed to construct his enormous underground structure. Although he allotted so much for the construction, he went way over his intended budget. Worrying about this seemed foolish, given the fact that money would be worthless once his plan was put into full effect. The rest of the bunker housed numerous labs, a fully operating cafeteria with chefs, many rooms converted into numerous bedrooms for most of the current staff living underground. It also had an extensive fitness center, complete with a sauna, steam room and an Olympic sized swimming pool. There was a warehouse completely stocked with non-perishables. Five gallon bottles of water were stacked from floor to ceiling with enough to last a minimum of two years at the least. There was a recreation room with a one hundred and twenty foot flat screen television and theatre chairs that housed at least one hundred people. Currently, Dr. Anglim had over two hundred employees on his payroll, half of which were living in the underground compound. Much of his source of income was contributed by the World Leaders he had recruited over the past few years to engage in his ultimate sacrifice of humanity. These leaders and dignitaries, along with their extended families, were to be granted survival once the massacre began. So basically the bunker was financed with almost all out of pocket expenses donated by countries around the continents. The finished bunker was designed precisely how Dr. Anglim imagined and very much to his liking. Now as he sat back in his oversized fully air conditioned and equipped office, he pondered what actions needed to take place next. As the eleven passengers were being led into the bunker, Dr. Anglim stared at the monitor. Of the twenty five monitors that were lined all along the walls, his eyes were fixated only on the one. The one that showed the unsuspecting group being marched into unknown territory. The mad doctor couldn't help but smile. A very large grin stretched from cheek to cheek. He took in a deep breath before exhaling out very slowly, and as the last person in line was led inside the bunker, his only thought was to 'let the games begin.'

32

Myleka was the last of the bunch to be put in the cell with the others. The guards took off the cuffs and left them to fend for themselves. As far as undoing their own blindfolds and gags, each one took no time in doing so. Every one of them spoke at the same time, bouncing questions off one another with no real answers to any of them. There were looks of concern on every face. Pete felt obligated to try to calm them all down so he held up his hand as he started, "Whoa, whoa, We all need to quiet down. One at a time. I know we're all scared but we need to remain calm. We can't show them how frightened we are even if that is the case. Let me think."

Tommy as usual had heard enough. "Let you think. We're all in this fucking mess because you didn't think quite enough. Again!"

Rita broke in, "Tommy, don't you dare blame your brother. He did what he thought was the right thing to do. And you young man better watch your language. How many times have I told…"

"Enough! I've heard enough! Who gives a crap about cursing? I'm sorry Rita. No disrespect to you, but it seems to me that our lives are all at stake here. Will it really matter if we swear or don't swear at this point?" Nick interrupted her. "Let's figure out how we can get out of this mess with our lives intact. I think we can assume who put us here, but it's the 'what are they planning on doing to us' that worries me."

Pete felt his heart racing as he listened to both his parents. He never should have involved them, but either way Dr. Anglim would have used his family as a means to lure him in.

"I'm sorry. I'm truly sorry that I've gotten all of us in this mess. I'll do whatever it takes to get us out of here in one piece. I'll sacrifice myself to Dr. Anglim if he will promise me all of your releases. I can't bear any more horrible treatment to any of you."

Maya ran over and threw her arms around him. "You'll do no such thing! Are you crazy? We knew what we were getting ourselves into. Now we have to put all our heads together and get ourselves out of this mess."

"She's right you know. When we took you five in with us, we became one group. We go through this together. Good or bad, we stick it out," Bill insisted. The others all listened as Pete explained what he had hoped might work in getting them free. As he was devising a plan, as foolish as it may be, the main doors leading down the hall to the large holding cell opened. With an armed soldier walking along each side of him, Dr. Anglim leisurely strolled down the hall, like he was taking a walk in the park. As he approached the bars of the large holding cell, he abruptly stopped.

"What a motley crew we have here. Actually sad and quite pathetic. Pietro, I would have given you more credit than this. Couldn't you do better in rounding up a better posse? Such a shame. Really. To think, you were my right hand guy. I taught you everything to make you irreplaceable, but that fell to shit. Didn't it? I'll have to make certain I vaccinate each of you to ensure your, shall I say, demise in time."

Standing too close for comfort by the bars, he didn't have time to react as two hands grabbed him by his lab coat and pulled him face first up against them.

"You fucking bastard! I'll kill you with my own bare hands if I have to. You lay one hand on any of us and you'll see..." Tommy shouted and was stopped mid-sentence as he continued to pull the doctor into the metal bars. The doctor was unable to break loose. His face instantly bruised from the force. Trying to keep his cool, you could see the brief moment of panic written all across his now swollen face. Seeing this, the soldiers reacted immediately. Before he knew what was happening, one of the soldiers took his rifle and slammed it down on Tommy's left wrist, which instantly had him release his grasp on the doctor. The other soldier used the butt of his rifle to aim it at Tommy's head. The impact from the blunt strike knocked Tommy out cold, causing the others to gasp as Tommy's body hit the floor. Witnessing the brutal beating her son had just taken, Rita, too, fainted and was caught by Nick as her body went limp and fell to the ground as well.

33

Pete stood there motionless and speechless. Maya held onto his hand pulling him in toward her. Karin rushed over to attend to Tommy while Nick cradled his wife in his lap, waiting for her come to. Laureen shuffled over to Myleka and hugged her, as Bill went to help aid Karin. Linh and Khang also made their way over to one another and just stared at the mayhem that just occurred. Dr. Walter Anglim stepped back away from the prison bars and rubbed his right cheek where the bruise was most evident. Before turning away to leave the group in disarray, he made a comment sure to chill them all to the bone. "Within the next twenty-four hours I'll have you all vaccinated with my own personal vaccine. Oh the pure joy! Once this is done, the end will be oh so near, and nothing any of you can do can stop me." A roar of laughter echoed and remained in the hollow hall as he was ushered out by the two soldiers. Nothing but the sound of the laughter remained, as the eleven people were left speechless.

34

Walter said his good nights to the soldiers that basically saved his life. With a promise of something so beneficial to the guards who prevented a near fatal tragedy, left them smiling from cheek to cheek anticipating their good fortune. Turning the corner, Dr. Anglim took an elevator in the bunker two levels down from where he held his prized possessions. He couldn't wait to begin his torment on each individual of Peter's group. He would break Peter one way or another to gain the access required to continue his slaughter of human life. Dr. Anglim counted his blessings that Peter was not killed in the cabin explosion. He wished Peter dead and did everything short of killing him himself, but by the stroke of good fortune, Peter survived all of his attempts. In hopes of possibly tracking Peter's next move, Dr. Anglim knew what needed to be done next. So, shortly after the explosion, he raided the Palumbo home himself. He didn't find any indication of his future whereabouts. However, after confiscating all of Peter's existing files on his personal laptop, he came across an encrypted formula. To his shocking surprise, there were many notes indicating the continued termination of all remaining population under fifty years of age and how it could be prevented. It also appeared that a specific calculation was installed into his hard drive to automatically create a virus to stop the spread of daily death.

This infuriated him. Dr. Anglim may have confiscated the vial which held the serum that could reverse the effects of his deadly vaccine, but another larger obstacle had to be dealt with. There were still hundreds of vials of the life-saving serum safely tucked away in a securely locked vault within his underground compound. These vials could potentially save millions of innocent lives. The doctor couldn't believe his complete foolishness in trusting what he thought was a future successor to his entire newly created universe. Peter, who at the time, seemed to be on board with the beginnings of Walter's plan, created his very own code that could stop the progression of the extinction of each age category once the age requirement hit the half way mark. At one point, Dr. Anglim was extremely proud of Peter's accomplishments in aiding him in his ultimate plan. Never did he imagine that this could come back and destroy all his hard work that took decades to create. He needed to get to his sanctuary and fast. In order to exit the elevator to enter his apartment, he needed to press a code to have access into his kingdom.

The doors closed and the elevator slowly descended. He reached his floor and the doctor punched in the four digit code allowing the doors to open. Walter stepped out on Level 4 and straight into his underground penthouse. Paradise awaited him. The thousand gallon fish tank was the first thing you saw upon walking in the spacious foyer. There were tropical fish of every origin and color. Coral reefs were scattered among the bottom of the aquarium allowing certain fish to blend in with them. Visitors would spend countless minutes staring at the wide variety of exotic aquatic fine specimens. After passing through the foyer, one would enter the oversized living room with the leather L-shaped couch with recliners attached on both ends. The loveseat and matching chair with an ottoman adorned the room. A seventy-five inch flat screen television with stereo sound was attached above the electric fireplace. The fireplace set the whole ambiance of the room. Dr. Anglim touched his cellphone and a fire was immediately ignited. He walked to the right of his living room and stepped around the island of his expansive kitchen. In contrast to a mostly dark colored living room, the kitchen was done in total white. The island countertop was a white granite speckled with traces of brown and every major appliance was pure white. The double convection oven served his every purpose as he was a self-taught chef. The rest of the kitchen showcased the glamour of an old Hollywood kitchen with the current flair of today's ultra-modern colors. Just down a very wide hallway, at the end was the master bedroom and adjoining master bathroom, which was larger than some people's homes. His walk in closet could fit a full-sized automobile. His style of taste was exquisite, along with his vast collection of designer suits and shoes. On those constant instances where he had a stint as a lecturer in front of hundreds of medical personnel, Dr. Anglim was always dressed to the nine. On more than one occasion he graced the cover of a highly visible medical magazine such as Health Magazine. It was within the spread of such an article that he was always asked about his fine choices in how impeccable his fashion taste was. Ensuring that he was never questioned about the possibility of wearing the same outfit twice, Walter purchased a new suit for every conference. Off each side of the wide spread hallway and before the master suite, were two other bedrooms each more glamorous then the other. These two bedrooms were barely used and the doors were mostly kept locked since no visitors were ever invited to spend an evening. On most walls were original paintings from famous artists from all around the world. Each room garnished a certain theme that highlighted every individual portrait. Walter took great pride in his underground dynasty. It was a progress well worth in the making. Immediately, Dr. Anglim kicked off his loafers and walked over to his fully stocked bar that was to the left of the living room. The mahogany bar matched the décor of the dining room. The large mahogany dining room table set for eight but never occupied by more than doctor himself, had eight matching chairs with plush seating. The china closet was eighteenth-century and was sculptured by the likes of Michelangelo himself. As he reached under the bar where he kept his glasses, he decided on Johnnie Walker Blue Label to quench his thirst. He took a rocks tumbler and poured a neat drink of the scotch. After the past few days, a stiff drink was precisely in order to ease his unwanted tension. All was going accordingly except for the pesky thorn in his side, better known as Peter. Dr. Anglim had once again reassured his world allies that all was going as planned and the extinction of each age group would continue daily. As of just this past noon, every eighty nine year old through eighty-five year old was greeted by the grim reaper whether they liked it or not. Mass hysteria reigned in every part of the world. The economy of the entire planet no longer prevailed as people fled, boarded, or holed up in their homes for the inevitable to take place. This brought a huge smile on the evil doctor's face. By the month's end, only the supreme would prevail. He would be the ruler of all that remained. All he needed to proceed was to break the code that Peter created and all of mankind would succumb to their ultimate demise. Upon polishing off his first neat Johnnie Walker Blue, Walter went into his bedroom where he proceeded to disrobe. After neatly placing today's clothes on his White Carlisle Upholstered Chaise, he went into his armoire to choose his nightly wear.

He fumbled through at least six very expensive pairs before settling on what he felt were his most comfortable. He took them out of the dresser. Carefully and with such precision he donned them. Realizing he had left his loafers in the living room, he stepped into his black Dolce and Gabbana slippers. The cost for his nightwear was equivalent to an average middle-class American's monthly salary. Satisfied with his comfort and current appearance, he decided on a second glass of scotch. He poured the neat tumbler and asked Alexa to play some soft classical music. He sat down and within a few minutes polished off the second drink. He quickly stood and went to grab the bottle of Blue Label. Again, he refilled the tumbler and took a big gulp of the exquisite tasty liquor. Rather than leave the bottle on the bar, he took it with him as he sat down on the couch. It was much easier and quicker to refill the glass from this vantage point. Dr. Anglim had a bad day and was hoping the future days would be brighter. He kept drinking until the third pour was gone. As he tilted the now half full bottle, he refilled the tumbler for the fourth and final scotch. His head finally felt fuzzy and warm. His thought process became hazy and his mind began to truly relax. He needed this break from reality. Too much was happening too fast, and all he wanted was this to end and for his new life to begin. He longed for much simpler times where he could be in complete control of all that remained. Dr. Anglim barely finished the drink as his hand fell to his side and the tumbler hit the floor and shattered. The smashing of the glass on the hardwood floor didn't even rouse him from his stupor. His whole body tilted and landed flat out across the couch where he went into a deep sleep, a sleep where dreams and nightmares stayed far, far, away. In place were memories of a long ago past, a time when he truly felt loved. He longed for that love again and hadn't felt it in such a long time that he lost track of how many decades had passed since he felt the warmth and love that only a mother could provide. A mother whose life was cut short at the hands of the only other person that may have loved him as well, in his own twisted and demented way. The person he never would have called his father if he knew what the outcome of his life would be.

35

*T*his was one of the first memories of many that the boy could never erase. All the young boy of eight felt was a sharp slap to the back of his head, sending him flying face forward. If it weren't for the fast reflexes from the boy's mother, he would have surely hit his head into the living room wall. The boy's mother barely had time to react as she grabbed the boy's arm and pulled him into her. She wrapped her arms tightly around his lean body, securing him in a protective manner. "Leave him ALONE! He didn't do anything other than grab you your slippers as you asked. Why must you torture us?" The mother pleaded. Laughing, the boy's father lifted his beer to his lips but not before chiding her. "Torture? Is that what you think I'm doing? I'm just trying to knock some sense into the kid before he grows up to be a sissy boy softened by the likes of you. Now go fetch me some dinner! And not some shit like you made the other night."

Antonnette, the boy's mother, guided her son from the living room straight into the kitchen of their four-bedroom *family ranch. The house was purchased right before the birth of their only child, the child she had and always would hold near and dear to her heart. Her mere existence was to nurture him, and unfortunately protecting him was also required. She went over to the simple oven and opened the door to check on the meatloaf she prepared for dinner. It was the father's favorite meal, one she cooked a hundred times over the years. Satisfied it was nearly done, she lowered the flames under the mashed potatoes cooking on the stovetop. The corn simmered in the pot next to it and she shut the flame off. As she turned to grab the silverware, Antonnette saw her reflection in the window above the kitchen sink. Her left eye still stung from the punch it received two nights ago for the sirloin steak she overcooked. She should have known the steak was too well done for her husband, but helping Walter with his math homework took precedence, and the time just slipped away. Knowing she could never cook another steak fast enough, she sautéed onions and mushrooms and covered the toughened meat to camouflage the crispness. The husband delighted in his first bite before realizing how tough the meat was. Pretending he was savoring each bite by smiling, he leaned over toward Antonnette who had just finished putting a split piece of sirloin with mashed potatoes and corn on her and her son's plates. Thinking she was given a break she leaned in to meet him half way as he continued smiling. Without a warning, he lifted his fist and punched her square in the eye sending her head backwards from the force. "You think I'm some kind of imbecile? Like I wouldn't notice just how* overcooked this steak is. You ruined a good piece of meat you stupid piece of shit! Covering it up with last minutes onions and mushrooms so I wouldn't see the meat. You really must think I'm an asshole don't ya? Well, let me set the record straight. You'd be better off telling me upfront rather than hide it. Your punishment would be less harsh if you were truthful. Now get off that fat ass of yours and grab me another beer. Actually make that two. My knuckles kinda hurt from that punch. And as for you sissy boy, one word out of that mouth of yours and you and your mother will have matching eye coloring. Get my drift?" Snapping out of her trance, she softly rubbed her hand over the black and blue bruise. She almost had a panic attack as she lost track of time. She hurried back over to the oven and turned off all the knobs. Glancing again at the meatloaf her heart rate slowed when she realized it was cooked exactly how her husband liked it. With trembling hands, she took out two matching oven mitts and reached in to take it from the rack. As she placed it on top of the stove she turned around and what she saw made her heartrate spike again. Walter held two beers in his little hands, as if to let her know either way they were doomed. Either he would drink too much, which she hoped was the case because nine out of ten times he would pass out on the sofa. If he drank too much but not nearly enough, his temper would surely flair up and only God knew what would happen when that was the case.

36

*Life for Antonnette and Walter wasn't always lived in fear.
In fact, much happier times were lived when Antonnette
first met her husband and eventually married him. He professed
his never ending love for her time and time again and on
more than one occasion told her he could never live without
her. Soon after their short courtship, they eloped and nine
months to the day, baby Walter was born. Antonnette's husband
was a traveling salesman and made a very lucrative salary
selling vacuums door-to-door. Within a short time, he had
risen up the ladder and was the number one salesman of the
eastern seacoast. Life was good for the Anglims. So good that
before their six month anniversary, the couple had went house
hunting. Knowing that their first child would be born shortly,
they settled on a four-bedroom ranch style home with three
additional bedrooms to be filled with plenty of children that
Antonnette's husband longed for. Longed for but never fulfilled.*

37

*L*ittle Walter was showered with an abundance of love and longed for nothing. Anything his little heart desired was fulfilled by his parents. His father's income was substantial enough to afford anything they wanted. The happy threesome were ready to expand. So right after Little Walter's first birthday the couple was ready to be fruitful and multiply. At first, they both thought that it was normal for a second pregnancy to take a bit longer to conceive. However, after three months went to six months and still no missed period, tension was starting to build.

Antonnette was always greeted with a warm smile and a gentle hug whenever her husband came home from work. As of lately she watched as her husband entered the house with barely a simple hello. Whenever he returned from a business trip he liked to surprise her with a small gift from whatever state he had visited to sell his vacuums. Usually a 'token of his love' as he liked to say to her. The last two trips he came back empty handed and not even a mention of how the trip went either. His demeanor was slowly turning into a stranger to Antonnette.

This bothered her immensely but she soon realized there was nothing she could do. All she could hope and pray for was that sooner rather than later, the race of the sperm to the egg would happen.

38

L ittle Walter's second birthday was fast approaching. What should have been a festive time in the Anglim household was anything but. Time spent in the bedroom lovemaking rather than sleeping was fast becoming hostile. Antonnette who once was passionate, was now totally sub- servient. Her husband who used to take his time and please her as much as himself, now treated her like an animal made to obey. Where they once took their time, now it was forced and rushed. It had become more of a chore rather than the act of lovemaking. She was laid flat on her stomach on their bed and was subjected to brutal entry from behind. This was out of the ordinary, as they were both accustomed to the missionary position for so many years. Staring into each other's eyes as they made love was very satisfying for the two of them. On several occasions they climaxed together from the passion they shared and the rhythm they matched. Now as she lay face down in their mattress, she silently prayed this whole ordeal was over. With his hand pressed firmly on the back of her neck and his other hand pinning both *of her hands behind her, the pain was unbearable. His thrusts were forceful and did not stop until he reached his orgasm. In the past he would always make sure she climaxed as well, but he no longer cared whether she did or not. The sex was rough and as short lived as both of their lives would soon become.*

39

*A*fter they both had went for numerous tests, it was concluded that her husband was to blame for the delay in Antonnette not bearing a child again because of his low sperm count. Following the diagnosis, years of mental and physical abuse occurred. He no longer could face Antonnette as the man he once was and resorted to knocking her around every chance he could. Where he once was a successful salesman, he now faltered in his yearly targets and goals. The doctors tried to rationalize with him that it could be due to the fact that he was under a lot of stress and pressure from his high demanding job to stay at number one. Regardless of their softening the blow to his male ego, he took it all out on Antonnette. Once he realized that she no longer flinched from his sudden fists to the face and body, he resorted to the next best thing, Walter.

40

"*You keep your hands off of him! Do you hear me? I don't care if you take all your frustrations out on me but don't you dare lay a finger on this boy! I am used to the beatings but I will not tolerate you hurting Walter. He doesn't deserve the abuse.*"

"*Oh, you poor, poor miserable little being. Don't you tell me who and what I'm allowed to do. Until you make the money and pay the bills, then you can speak up. So keep your damn mouth shut. Do I make myself clear?*" *Antonnette was just about to turn around and head for the kitchen when she felt his hand grab her forearm and twist her around to face him. Before she could react, he slapped her across the face. Her cheek instantly turned a crimson red. Walter, who was now a teenager of fifteen, charged at his father. He wasn't as agile as his old man though and missed him when his father darted out of the way. "Look at you two. How pathetic! You call yourself a man? All I see is a little boy. No, make that a momma's boy!" The father laughed as he pushed his son clearly out of the way.*

"And if you ever charge at me like that again, I'll break both of your legs. Now get the hell out of my way." Antonnette and Walter just stood there and watched as the evil man, better known as the husband and father, left them alone in the living room.

41

*H*ugging his mother and gently applying a cold compress to her swollen cheek, the young teenager spoke soothingly to the only person he truly loved more than life itself. "Mom, listen to me. Please look at me. You can't go on living your life with this tyrant. It will never get better, and you know better than I do that it will only get worse. His rage is out of control. He blames you for everything and anything. I'm not stupid. I know he blames you for not having any more children. You can't go on living like this. He'll wind up killing you and then I promise you I'll kill HIM!"

Seeing the glint of hatred in her son's eyes frightened Antonnette. She had never seen her son with such animosity towards the man he once worshipped and adored. She actually pitied her husband. Where he was once successful and highly regarded, he now tethered on the edge of losing his job. Since he had found out he was the one preventing the Anglim family from growing, he could not handle it. Now he even looked at the housewives he used to charm into buying a vacuum with *disgust in his eyes. If there was more than one child in the house, it infuriated him and most times the sale was lost. He couldn't hide his disdain for the families he once delighted in marketing his product. Over the course of the years his income drastically declined and there was barely enough to maintain the household.*

Now as they sat next to one another on the couch, she knew something had to be done. Before her son eventually became a man and outgrew his father in strength and endurance, she needed to take matters into her own hands. She wouldn't and couldn't let anything happen to the only person that mattered to her now. Walter was her reason for living and she would give up her life to protect him. He loved her just as much as life itself. Little did they both know in just a few short years, life would never be the same.

42

Throughout the years, his father's mood never brightened as he took more and more of his father's wrath in order to spare his mother the continued beatings. The more beers he consumed after arriving home, the more his fists swung freely. Depending on the severity of his father's temper resulted in the amount of blows he would suffer from that evening. It was becoming harder for Walter to attend school on a daily basis. More often than not, he would have his mom call the school office with one excuse after another to list him as absent. Most of the time, Walter hid as many of the bruises as best he could to not bring unwanted attention from his teachers. The few who had questioned him on a particular black and blue were convinced he was a typical, awkward, clumsy teenager upon listening to the many excuses he conjured up. As far as friends, he was a loner and spent all his free time at home where he felt his mother would be safer with him present. This is how Walter spent his high school days. A self-proclaimed loner who loved his mother to the ends of the earth, who at any cost would protect her to the last breath he took, until that one day in chemistry class when a light bulb went off in his head. Walter was prepared to turn off the switch that would end a violent person's life.

43

It was while he was a senior in high school and taking advanced organic chemistry that his plan came to mind. They were experimenting with rat poison and the many side effects of this undetectably fatal toxin. If mixed in with something of a stronger flavor, it could never be tasted. That was when he realized how he could kill his father. Never did he actually refer to him as his dad as that was a word used to reflect on the strong bond of love between a man and his son. The term father was more formal and felt a bit more standoffish, making his plan all the more easier. His father's favorite dish was his mom's Irish stew. It was a recipe passed down from his mother's great grandmother and from generation to generation, straight from Dublin, Ireland. Usually on stew night, the beatings were less forceful due to the fact that his father consumed many servings of the Irish stew that his mom perfected, and with a full belly it took more effort to enforce a brutal beating. So every Wednesday like clockwork, it was Irish stew night. Devising the plan was simple enough, but getting the rat poison into his dish unnoticed took some extra work. For years his mother always scooped their portions into bowls and served them around the dining room table. More often than not, Antonnette's husband was intoxicated by dinnertime. He spat curse words at both mother and son as he waited for his favorite weekly dish. Antonnette made sure her beloved son was seated and safe before placing the bowl down in front of him. With a bit of persuading he managed to convince her, "Mom, please sit down. Let me fix the bowls. You look tired. Between trying to keep the house clean, laundry done, food shopping and preparing all the meals, you need to rest. I'm capable of pouring the bowls. You sit and I'll do the rest."

Having been truly exhausted from her daily workload, Antonnette decided to succumb to his wishes instead of putting up a fight, so for the next few weeks she did just that. She sat down every Wednesday and let Walter cater to her, something that hadn't been done for her in years.

After devising his ultimate plan, Walter went to the local hardware store a few weeks later and asked the salesperson where they kept the rat poison, stating they were experiencing a pest control problem in their basement. After purchasing the deadly toxin, Walter snuck it into his room and shred the cubes into what appeared like strings of cheese, which was one of the ingredients in the stew. The first time he scooped up his father's portion of stew his hands were visibly shaking. He was extremely nervous and did his best to hide his nerves for fear that his father would lash out on him. He mixed in the poison

Vincent N. Scialo

and silently prayed it would be eaten by his father unnoticed, hoping his drunkenness would kill his taste buds and make it less likely to be detected. As he placed the bowl down in front of his father, he stepped back, but not before vicious words were unleashed. "Looky here, sissy boy has resorted to serving us our dinner. I knew you were a faggot from the first time I hit your ass." With plea in her eyes, his mom's stare told Walter to take the snide remarks in jest and ignore the maniac present at the table. If things continued the way they were heading, it was only a matter of time that he would be fired from his once golden ticket of employment. Where he once took pride in punctuality and out of town business trips to enhance his sales, he now woke up later each morning and travelled less and less each month. He was warned by the human resource department a number of times and notes to his file were documented ensuring that he would be fired if things continued the way they were. After shoving down his first serving, he gestured to his son, "I guess this is what your mother wants. She wants you to be a waitress. Whoop de fucking doo, my sissy boy has grown up and wants to be a girly waitress." He laughed as he wiped the stew from his lips on his shirtsleeve. Walter turned and walked back into the kitchen with a full smile on his face that only he could sense. As he scooped out a larger second portion, he reached into his dungarees and pulled out the small sandwich bag with the shredded rat poison. This time he was less shaky as he mixed the poison in with the Irish stew. If what the side effects of the continued rat poison guaranteed, it was only a matter of time before the head of the household met his maker. Walter again felt his cheeks expand into a smile. His father's maker would soon be eagerly awaiting in the depths of hell for this twisted demented man who had tortured his family enough.

44

Slowly the weeks progressed, the stew was consumed, and Walter's patience faltered. According to the dosage amounts of rat poison he had been mixing into the weekly stew, his father should have passed on by now. There were immediate signs though like skin rashes that appeared all over his body, and Walter knew the poison was working. His father constantly shouted out to his mother asking for her to treat them with ointments. This pleased Walter to no end, an end that was oh so near.

45

It was on a typical Saturday afternoon that Walter's life was about to change forever. He had just finished mowing the front and back lawns, which was part of his weekly required chores.

As he pushed the mower back and forth in a straight even line for fear that if it even appeared off center, he would once again suffer an unnecessary beating. His thoughts kept reflecting on the last few days. His father's health was quickly deteriorating. He had difficulty breathing and where he usually showed extreme strength in swinging his fists, he now showed apparent signs of weakness. In the middle of the night Walter could hear his father vomiting in the hallway bathroom as his mother stood over him with a cold washcloth pressed to his forehead. One morning there was a loud shout from his father which had Walter run directly to the bathroom. Upon looking into the open door he watched as his father spit blood into the bathroom sink and when he turned around to face him, his father's gums were bleeding. His mother insisted that he go to the emergency room, but he was too stubborn. When she pressed the issue too much, his father still had enough energy to smack her square in the cheek sending her flying across the room. This infuriated Walter all the more, but he kept his cool knowing the poison was in full effect.

Days turned into a few weeks and his father still kept on waking up each morning. Walter prayed for the day he wouldn't. His prayers were finally answered. It was on a bright sunny Saturday morning and Walter had just cleaned the mower and emptied out the grass bag, when he heard a life piercing scream come from his mom. Quickly he bolted straight from the garage and in the front door. His father was doubled over with one hand clutching his stomach and the other holding the bannister. Foam was dribbling from his father's mouth and blood had ran down his white t-shirt. Trying to keep his balance as he attempted to make his way down the stairs, all kinds of obscenities were uttered from his mouth. Language not suitable for any age was deafening to Walter's ears. "You did this to me you bitch! Just what have you been doing?" His mother pleaded with his father, "I swear I did nothing. I would never HURT you!" Walter watched in slow motion as his mother continued to scream at the top of her lungs just how much she loved this beast, better known as her husband.

"If I find out you've been lying to me, I'll fucking rip your throat apart. What the fuck was I even thinking? I should have killed you years ago before sissy boy was even born!" Saliva drooled down his chin.

Vaccinated

"How could you say such horrible things?" Trying to rationalize with this deranged individual, she continued "I'm your wife and for God sakes that's OUR son! How could you? I love you! I always have and always will regardless of the beatings you've given me." This baffled Walter. After years of witnessing and taking brutal beatings, his mom still had the capacity to love his father. She begged him to let her take him to the hospital to be treated but he refused her pleas. Instead, he said he needed to go to the local tavern that he often frequented to get away from this toxic family. Just last week he was let go of his job after years of the company overlooking his downfall in hopes of him rebounding. His father's life had spiraled out of complete control, and now his health was at the very worst. The company could no longer keep him on payroll. If there were serious health conditions involved, now was the time to let him go before unwanted expenses would also occur. Employees had noticed that his health was worsening every day and some were afraid they might catch what he had. Many complaints were issued to the owner of the vacuum company, and this was the final straw needed to release him of his responsibilities.

Walter was spotted by his father. There was pure hatred in his father's eyes as he saw him getting closer. Walter had had enough. He despised this man so much that he couldn't hold back any longer. Even if it meant dealing with the circumstances after his death, and mostly dealing with his mom who would never forgive him for what he was about to confess.

"Why? Can you just tell me why you hated mom and me so much when all we ever wanted was YOUR love? A small fucking smidgeon of love. Was that asking too much? So you know what old man? I'm the one you should be blaming and not mom. She had no idea of what I had planned for you these past few months. Jeez man, I must say you are built like an ox. The poison I've been scooping into your stew every week and the way you always had second helpings should have killed you weeks ago. Although the way you're looking now, I would say you're close to death's door. It's about time if you ask me. You had it coming for a while. No, actually for years if I'd have known how to do what I did now, back then. I'm ashamed to even say I have a father. You were never good to either of us and you deserve what you had coming to you."

His mother stopped in her tracks at the top of the staircase. Her face said it all. Shock, disbelief and even an ounce of fear was written across it.

"Please Walter, please tell me you didn't do this. He's your father."

Unable to hold back the laughter, Walter smirked "In name only mom. How could you defend his actions over the years? The beatings. The physical and mental abuse. How?"

"How? I did. I just did. But to poison him. I mean look at him. Walter. What did you do?"

Antonnette's husband's face contorted into rage. If looks could have killed, she was certain her only child would be dead.

"*I swear if I get my hands on you, you're DEAD. Do you hear me sissy boy, DEAD!*"

Determined to get down the flight of stairs to confront his son, he slowly took the first step down the staircase, when he went into a highly dangerous seizure. Certain it was brought upon by the sudden stress he just experienced, his whole body arched up and back and he lost his footing. Antonnette, sensing if she didn't do something and fast, her violent abusive husband may tumble to his death. She leaned forward but not before her husband let go of the bannister and grabbed onto her arm and pulled her down as he fell forward. They both tumbled down each step of the staircase flipping over one another as they did. Walter's father landed on his back. The blood that was spewing from his mouth had now backed up in his throat and caused him to choke to death on it. His mom however was also not quite so fortunate. Her neck caught on the pole of the very last rung of the bannister where it hit it so hard that her neck snapped and killed her instantly. All of this terror lasted a mere three minutes, but to Walter it felt like a lifetime. Pushing past his much deserved dead father, he dropped to his knees where he gently lifted his dead mom while cradling her in his arms for what felt like an eternity, all the while crying tears for this dead woman who he would never watch grow old.

46

S unlight rays beamed straight into the living room floor to ceiling windows and landed directly in Dr. Anglim's eyes. When he first opened them, he quickly shielded them from the blinding sun. At first he was dazed and confused and had a splitting headache. Images of his dead mother at the bottom of the stairs flooded his memory. It wasn't until he tried to sit up that thoughts of last night's activities came into focus. The first sign was the near empty bottle of scotch, followed closely by the broken shards of glass at his feet when he sat up on the couch. He wondered how things had gotten so bad that he resorted to almost polishing off a bottle of scotch by himself. Now as he scratched his crotch, thoughts came back to him in bits and pieces, thoughts he tried to push out of his mind completely but always reappeared when alcohol consumption was involved.

Stepping aside from the broken glass, he went down the hallway and into his master bedroom. The bed was meticulously made and hadn't been slept in. Glancing at the

Vaccinated

digital clock on the nightstand he noticed the time. It was already half past ten and in less than two hours the next age group would be extinguished by simply programming their date of birth by year into the main computer locked away in the lower hub of the underground fortress. He needed to do the three S's- shit, shower and shave all within the next thirty minutes or he may jeopardize the next block of unwilling sacrifices of life. Today he planned on terminating his largest group yet. Anyone from the age of eighty-four through seventy five would be eliminated by the press of a button verifying the codes necessary to complete this task. The doctor sat on the bowl to urinate rather than stand. After drinking as much fluid as he did, his bladder was full and it took a bit longer than normal to drain his stream of pee. He also preferred to shave before he showered. When he saw his reflection in the master bathroom, he took a double take. Staring back at him was a man he barely recognized. Where he once looked strong and vibrant, shadows of aging graced his face with wrinkle lines he never noticed before. As he carefully maneuvered the razor along his jawline, random thoughts of his past came back to haunt him. Quickly finishing up, he turned on the faucet inside the shower and waited while the temperature warmed up before stepping in. When the water felt hot enough, he leaned under the shower head and let the water cascade down his head and body. Trying to push away the painful memories of his past didn't work. As the stream of hot water hit his face, he thought of all the years after his parents' deaths.

He was an orphan at eighteen and had no family to take him in. There were no friends to hold him up at his parents' funerals. His mother's death was ruled an accident and while an autopsy on his father was performed and the results were deemed suspicious, no fingers were pointed his way. The police as well as the medical examiner's office felt pity for this fine young man who now had to face life on his own. After his father was terminated right before his untimely death, the insurance policy they had for him was null and void. Walter's only saving grace was that the mortgage was paid off. This was done while his father was on top of his game and the sales were exuberant. With only bad memories for most of his life while living in the house, he had no issues when a real estate agent approached him at the gravesite asking what his plans for his home were. The successful young realtor told him that the market was in favor of the seller since there was more demand than supply. Having gotten top dollar and a considerable amount over asking price due to a bidding war, Walter was financially secure. Four years of college and medical school to continue in scientific research didn't even put a dent in his life savings. Having found a new passion, Walter followed the stock market closely while in classes and made some very lucrative investments adding to his growing fortune. What he made in money, he lacked in love. Of all his few relationships over his earlier years, none had ever amounted to anything, since no woman could compare to his mother. Sexually, these women were deeply satisfying but emotionally there was no love strong enough to keep him from taking the relationship to the next level. Most women were left wondering what they could have done to end the relationship so swiftly and so cold. Many had pleaded for a second chance but were never given the opportunity. They were often left heartbroken and fragile going into their next courtship, which didn't affect Walter in the slightest. He carried on with life and missed his mother more and more with each passing day. Never forgiving himself for letting on about poisoning his father ultimately led to his mom's untimely passing. He wished he could turn back the clock and race up the steps to prevent his father from grabbing onto his mom. In many nightmares over the years, he watched his mother tumble time and time again and heard the sound of her neck breaking. This caused him to lash out at most people for no apparent reason other than to blame them for his mom's death. Passing the blame made it easier for him. As the years passed him by, his hostility toward most individuals for no apparent reason increased. He found on several incidents that bitterness crept into his voice and usually kept most people at bay. The ones that were brave enough to confront him were usually left shuffling away with their tail between their legs. Walter had zero tolerance for incompetent people and quickly put them in their place. Leaning against the shower walls with his arms outstretched, the hot water continued to run over his face. Trying to push away life's past wasn't easy. So many painful memories led him to this stage of his life. Finding how much he truly hated people pushed him further along to start a plan to leave only a superior race left worldwide. With a lucrative and scientifically enhanced organization that he created from scratch, Epigen Hyperspace came with a high price. Exhaustive research, persuasive bargaining, powerful negotiations, and a determination beyond all reasoning placed him at the top of his game. A deadly game at the least. Survival of the fittest deemed worthy by only he himself. Time was of the essence and the clock was quickly ticking. He was afraid he would fall behind schedule if his thoughts continued to take over his mind. He wouldn't let that happen under any such circumstances. Now as his plan was in its final stages, he pushed off the walls of the shower and grabbed the bar of soap. Hoping to wash away the sweat and uncleanliness accumulated from yesterday, he was relentlessly scrubbing away the dirt of his past too.

47

Satisfied in programming the latest batch of perishable people, Dr. Anglim completed the zoom call with all the dignitaries and head of countries. It was one o'clock in the afternoon and the world was in utter turmoil. The United States of America was not united anymore. Every citizen feared for themselves or their loved ones. There was no telling how large the gap of ages would be from day to day and there was no fleeing the outcome. President Neubert made his daily State of the Union speech trying to reassure the American people that a remedy of some sort would stop the rate of deaths in the very near future. Just how near he wasn't able to verify. People didn't believe or want to hear what he had to say anymore. Most of them wanted to spend whatever time they had left with their loved ones. Companies were closing at rates too fast to comprehend. No one was willing to go into work anymore as every moment of every day was precious. Hospitals were overwhelmed with people hoping if they brought their loved ones in that they would be able to somehow save them. Unfortunately hospitals were understaffed too and couldn't provide sufficient care. The whole of the universe had taking a turn for the worse. The wrong turn with no way of coming back in the right direction.

48

Knowing just how much chaos reigned in the world pleased Dr. Anglim. As he sat in his leather high back Gates Genuine office chair with his hands behind his head, he watched the monitors that held his prized possessions. Each and every one of the eleven people would play a part in the next stage of his game. Only one player though was needed to complete the pattern needed to finish off mankind. The other ten were pawns readily available for extinction if the most important player wouldn't cooperate.

49

The five of them sat in the private dining area with the mad doctor. Indulging in a meal fit for a king, they ate in silence like they had never seen such a feast of enormous proportions. There was almost every food imaginable and desired. From eggs Benedict to a six foot American hero with all the sides to filet mignon cooked to perfection, their appetites were quenched having eaten non-stop for close to an hour. It was time to set the stage.

"So, has Peter confided in any of you regarding his secret plan to try and stop me?" Each of them continued to consume large quantities of food, ignoring what was just asked of them. The doctor didn't like to be ignored. He slammed his fist on the table and some of the plates that held food bounced up. The five heads that had been busy swallowing down their food, stopped and looked at the hand that just fed them. Linh, Khang, Laureen and Myleka looked over at Bill with pleading eyes. Bill, who felt like their protector, spoke first. "And why the hell would we tell you, even if we did know, which we don't. From what I have gathered, you are the culprit behind all this mayhem and destruction. You deserve to pay for what you are doing."

Laughing and placing both hands on the table to lift himself up, the Doctor smiled. "Yes, I am the what was the word you used, culprit. Yes, culprit behind all this. And look what I have accomplished so far. Total annihilation of worthless human beings. Kudos to me! And now it seems like you lot are just as worthless." Doctor Anglim montioned to the five soldiers who were patiently waiting for their next orders. With a point to the five individuals, the soldiers knew exactly what to do. Each soldier grabbed one of the five and lifted them off their chairs. Laureen who grabbed her daughter's hand held back and spoke her mind. "You piece of spineless shit! I hope you rot in hell for this."

"Momma, please. Don't say anything else. God only knows what he'll do to you. Please momma. Stay quiet."

"You people are a pathetic bunch. Of no use to anyone, especially me. If I were you I would work on getting Peter to give up the information I need, or the next time you're in front of me it will be a lot worse. And I mean a lot!"

50

Doctor Anglim waited until after dinner to resort to what needed to be done next. There was no more time to sugar coat what he needed most. Rather than waste his time with Peter's parents, brother and girlfriend, he devised a different plan of action. Peter, once and for all, had to give him the code to continue with his elimination process. He needed to break the group up and threaten Peter that if he didn't, sacrifices would be made. First he would bring Pete's father, brother, and the loud mouth Bill into the examination chamber located at the base of the bunker. After would be Pete's mother, girlfriend, the outspoken African American woman and the other woman who he since forgotten about. Then it would be the sister and brother along with the youngest girl among them. One from each group would be sentenced to a lethal injection until Peter cooperated to the fullest. As he was just about to summon the men from the group a totally different idea popped into his head. Instead of using a soldier to get the person who may be able to solve all this unnecessary stress, he took out his cell phone and texted Melanie to come immediately to his office. He needed a mental break and Melanie was just the fix. Her cheery disposition and optimistic approach to life always lifted his spirits. Knowing her since she was a little girl and watching her mature into a beautiful young woman truly invigorated him. She was a breath of fresh air in a damp, dank and dismal world. Within the first seven minutes of the confirmed text to see the doctor, Melanie knocked on his door before entering.

"Come in. Why hello Melanie, you look as beautiful as ever. I have a favor or more or less a plan I need your assistance with. I promise you the reward for helping me get what I need will outweigh all your future wants and needs."

Melanie, who just turned twenty-four last week, listened intently to what the doctor requested. Her father worked for Dr. Anglim for the past twenty years and brought his only child on board once he knew what was in store for civilization. He entrusted her with the doctor's future plans when he felt she was ready to be able to fully absorb the aftermath. Melanie loved her parents and he knew she would do anything to be with them. A stunning blonde with green eyes and a figure that caught the eyes of most men and envy from many a woman, she stood at five feet seven and gave the impression she was a lot taller. Walter waved her in and motioned his hand for her to take a seat across from him. After offering her a glass of his finest champagne, which she gladly accepted, he explained in great detail what he expected of her with no not being an option.

After two additional glasses of champagne, Melanie left his office feeling slightly lightheaded but also very determined to succeed with what the doctor ordered. First thing on her agenda was to go down to the holding cell of the eleven captives and escort Maya to the doctor. She was to kiss up to her and win her confidence, much like they were two girlfriends who went way back. Melanie went with four soldiers to the cell and waited while they opened the numerous locks to let her in with the group. The living conditions were deplorable as far as she was concerned. Cots were grouped together by family relations from what she could tell. At least they were able to use the lavatory down the hall in privacy. Showers were limited, but they were provided with three full meals a day. Her father had filled her in on these minor details as she questioned their arrival and what exactly their purpose was. Now as she walked in among the group looking for Peter's girlfriend, she locked eyes with Tommy for the first time. In all her years of dating and the very few relationships she did have, she never knew what the expression 'love at first sight' meant. Now as she stood there motionless and gazing into the deepest darkest eyes she had ever seen, she almost forgot what her purpose was. Trying to break the locked gaze she shared with this man she had never laid eyes on before, she desperately needed to do what was asked of her. Tommy, sensing the immediate attraction he also felt, took advantage of the situation and the chance to speak to the most beautiful girl he had ever seen. "Excuse me for asking, but how in the world does a girl like you wind up in a place like this?"

Dumbfounded by the question, but wanting to answer this handsome guy, she did her best to reply, "I beg your pardon. This is my life. I've helped my dad here for years until they brought me on board to do medical research in areas of my expertise from schooling." Forgetting there were fourteen people watching this love connection unfold, Melanie, flustered from the three glasses of champagne, continued, "Is that any way to get a girl's attention? I mean shouldn't you have introduced yourself first before asking about my employment here. Seems to me that I should be asking you the same question." Tommy walked over and put his hand out and was surprised by just how fast Melanie took hold of his. "I'm Tommy Palumbo and the pleasure is all mine."

"I'm Melanie Dubois and likewise." Feeling her face flush from the touch of his hand, she snapped out of the trance and remembered her purpose for being there. "Perhaps if the circumstances were different we could have been friends. Unfortunately for now I'm here to see Maya. I have some urgent business to discuss between us girls. Looks like girl power is the theme for tonight. So, Maya if you'll join me I promise I'll show you a different side to this place. A side nearly not so gloomy and depressing. So let's get out of here and I'll get you some much needed space for the time being." Taking Maya by the hand and leading her from the holding block, she once again glanced over to Tommy and smiled. Maya, on the other hand, looked over to Peter who nodded, hoping to let her know that all would be okay. Maya, scared and uncertain, held tightly to Melanie's hand as she was led out of the cell and into the unknown.

51

"Are you insane? You want me to betray my boyfriend so you can wipe out all of the people that are left in the world. What makes you think I would agree to such a morbid request?"

Fifteen minutes ago Melanie dropped Maya off in the IT room that housed more than one hundred monitors with images from all over the world on different screens. Dr. Anglim sat in the middle of the room at the grandest of desks that enabled him to swivel his chair to face each monitor. He instructed Maya to take the seat directly in front of him. He watched as she played with her hands by rubbing them together in circles. Letting her sit there in silence for a few minutes before he demanded her assistance put her more on edge. When he finally asked her to seduce Peter in order to coax the information needed, Maya lost it. He offered the Presidential Suite in the bunker that was given to any dignitary or world leader upon their visit. The suite was assigned its own butler to fulfill any whim the dignitary would desire. Walter had instructed the suite be filled with the finest foods and best champagne. Maya was to make sure that she seduced Peter either sexually or by intoxication. If both were needed then the results might be given up more readily. Having just listened to Maya's tantrum was exactly what the good doctor expected. What girlfriend would betray her loving boyfriend of so many years? Her so called future husband. That was why he summoned her to the IT room. As she sat staring off into space waiting for him to answer her recent hissy fit, all across the monitor screens images of a familiar family appeared. In each frame of every computer were her parents and three siblings doing various things in their home on the island, Bermuda. Where just a few short moments ago she stared off into space, now her eyes were glued to every monitor with fear evident in them. Shaking uncontrollably, although the temperature was far from cold and with a quiver in her voice, she pleaded, "Why do you have my family plastered on every screen?" Knowing beforehand what his intentions were she continued, "Please don't harm them." Realizing it was falling on deaf ears by just looking at his facial expression, Maya panicked. "Oh God! I see where this is going. If I don't get what you want from Peter, you plan on..."

"Such a smart girl are we? I thought I would have to paint a full picture of what I had planned if you failed miserably of my request, but I must have shorted you on intelligence. Maya, oh sweet Maya. You have tonight to get what I desperately need or how shall I put it?" With a click of a button on the keyboard, every screen went blank and all images of her loving family vanished into thin air. It was as if there was no evidence that her family of five ever existed. At that precise moment Maya realized that if she failed the evil doctor, they would be eliminated by default.

52

Peter didn't trust the scenario he was now in. His instincts were on high alert. Maya returned to the holding cell just briefly enough to whisk him away with her, before he had a moment to process what was taking place. She was escorted back by the young girl named Melanie, who again exchanged lustful glances in the direction of his brother Tommy. Melanie, along with two soldiers this time, stood by. All of this took place in seconds upon Maya's arrival back. She whispered in his ear and the next thing he knew, he was being led away to what appeared to be a suite fit for a king. They were greeted at the entrance to the suite by a very tall man who said he was to be referred to as Wyatt, and he was at their beck and call. He opened the door to the suite and Maya and Peter followed closely behind. Inside the foyer was paradise and every room within radiated tranquility and pure eloquence. On the glass dining room table was an assortment of various cheeses, meats, fruits and desserts. Off to the right of the table were three buckets filled with ice and Louis Roederer Cristal champagne sticking out from the top. Peter knew something was not right and could barely restrain from questioning Maya the moment Wyatt left them alone. "Would you mind telling me exactly where you went and what went down when Melanie took you from our cell?" Maya didn't answer. Not wanting to ruin the moment, she walked over to the table and started to fix them both plates. Noticing she wasn't about to explain anything, Peter who was ravished himself, popped open a bottle of the very fine champagne and poured two chilled glasses. For the next thirty minutes they drank and ate like they hadn't seen food in years. Neither of them spoke a word as they devoured the delicious spread left for them. They also polished off two of the three bottles of champagne like it was water. Having full stomachs left them satisfied for the moment. Breaking the silence, Peter again asked her why and how they ended up where they were. Rather than answer him again, she walked over to Peter and wrapped her arms tightly around his neck and pulled him in for a long awaited kiss.

Without hesitating, Peter buzzed himself from the champagne, returned the kiss with fierce passion. Feeling Maya's arms around his neck stimulated feelings he hadn't felt in months since he fled the laboratory. Leaving the feast and expensive champagne behind and knowing what he was about to do next even under the current circumstances, felt all wrong. Peter took her hands off his neck and led her directly into the bedroom. The king sized bed was decorated with sheer white lace draped all around it, giving the bed an innocent appearance. Picking her up, he carried her into the room and placed her gently on the bed. With a ferocity like two primal animals in heat, they tore at one another's clothes until they were both naked. Neither of them let go of the other and Peter jumped up on the bed and lay directly on top of Maya. With their lips locked together, Peter lifted her legs onto his shoulder and gently entered her. Within seconds their bodies moved in perfect rhythm. Peter thrusted in and out in sync with her movements. Seconds turned into minutes and both of them were sweating profusely. They hadn't made love in months and the desire was intense. Maya grabbed his buttocks and pulled him in closer to match her strides. Lifting her vagina up into the air, she thrashed about under his weight, enjoying every moment of passion. For nearly fifteen minutes they clawed at one another all along gasping for air in their constant lovemaking. Finally, together as one, they climaxed. Flipping over on his back and out of breath, Peter put his arms under his head and relaxed for the first time in quite a while. Forgetting what he had even asked Maya prior to their lovemaking didn't seem to bother him at the moment. The only thing that truly mattered was the unspoken love he felt for Maya. Nothing could ever break them apart. Totally exhausted he felt Maya lean over and place her head on his chest. Within seconds she was fast asleep, and before he even had time to rethink what he wanted to ask her, he too passed out and was sleeping.

53

Maya tossed and turned in her sleep. Twice she woke up and didn't know where she was until she looked over and saw Peter lying next to her. Then it all came crashing back. Meeting the mad doctor, the gourmet spread of food and champagne, the intense session of steamy sex with Peter and her final ultimatum. Peter's code or her family's demise. Breaking out in a cold sweat, Maya quickly rose from the bed and briskly made her way to the enormous bathroom where she splashed cold water on her face. She needed to convince Peter to go along with what she needed to give to the doctor or her family would pay the price, and the price was not right, in fact it was totally wrong.

54

Peter rolled over and spread his arm out to touch Maya. When his arm came away empty, he sprung up from the bed. Naked, he went in search of Maya. Seated in the exquisite living room, he caught sight of her. She was wrapped in a fluffy white bathrobe tied at her waist. It looked as if she had been crying. She dabbed at her eyes with a Kleenex. Peter quietly approached her. He coughed as to not startle her and she turned her head around to glance his way. "Sweetheart, is everything okay? It looks like you've been crying. What's going on? You know you can tell me anything."

Sniffling and blowing her nose, she wrapped her arms around her waist, "Peter, last night was so special. We haven't made love like that in I can't even remember the last time. I love you more than words could ever express and I need you to listen to me. Listen to me closely. You HAVE to give me the code to disengage the encryption you have blocking all access to people under fifty. You just have to."

Peter stood there naked and in disbelief of what he just heard. Maya wanted him to give her the life-saving code he created behind his mentor's back. It took him precise analytical precision to master what he accomplished in such a short period of time. When all his hard work fell into place and he was able to block the remaining sacrifice of human life below fifty years of age, he knew he had accomplished his greatest gift yet, and now Maya wanted him to hand over the code as if she were asking for a family recipe. Plain and simple. Yet deep down in his heart, Peter knew he would never give it up. Even if his own life depended on it, and that's exactly what it did.

55

Forgetting their passion from hours ago, Maya stood facing Peter. "Listen to me. I'm only going to say this one more time. I NEED the CODE and I NEED it NOW! Don't you get it? We're all screwed either way. Why prolong the inevitable?"

"Maya, where is this coming from? What did they do to you when they took you away for a while yesterday? I'll never give up what I worked so hard to create. How could you even ask me to do such a thing? This is just the beginning. If I can stop the doctor from killing off half the age groups under fifty and if I can get my hands on the anti-virus formula vials, we can get millions of people vaccinated correctly where they can never fear that their lives could be terminated on any given day. I HAVE to get those vials! You are not helping asking me to destroy all that I accomplished."

Tears streaked down her cheeks, and Maya begged. "Please for the love of God, just tell me the fucking code!"

Peter never heard Maya use the 'f' word and this caught him off guard. There was more behind her begging than she was letting on to. If only she would be truthful and stop badgering him with no explanation. Frustrated and fearful for her family's fate, Maya spun around and headed for the bathroom door. Without uttering another word, she gathered her clothes off the floor by the bed and entered the bathroom where she would shower and dress. She needed to come up with a different way to save her family. She couldn't just blurt it out to Peter. Five lives in comparison to millions would not suffice Peter. Of course he would feel horrible if he couldn't save them from certain death and probably would never be able to live with himself for doing so. Peter quickly followed her in an effort to put an end to what was a perfect evening. As he was just about to stop her from going into the bathroom, she took no time in ensuring her distance as she slammed the door in his face.

56

Showered and now fully dressed, Maya unlocked the bathroom door. She tiptoed out in hopes of not having another confrontation with Peter. Unfortunately, he plopped himself down right outside the door and jumped up as soon as she exited. Startled and not strong enough to continue the battle she was sure to lose, Maya did the only thing she could think of to get away fast. She called out to Wyatt who instantly appeared as if he was a genie from a bottle, and in no time flat, he led her out of the suite, leaving Peter behind in the dust.

57

Dr. Anglim had cringed during the lovemaking. Up until then he spied on their every move. Now however, he had shut down the camera in the bedroom, not wanting to see two naked bodies tossing about. He did keep the listening device up to full volume so he wouldn't miss a word of their conversation. Between the panting, heavy breathing and ultimately the combined orgasm, not much was discussed. Although he wasn't able to bring himself to watch them in live action, in his own twisted and demented way he found his hand gently stroking his penis to the sounds of a young couple near completion. He was aroused and mad at himself for allowing this. If it weren't that he had a full day tomorrow and needed sleep, he just might have jerked himself off. As it was, he didn't want to clean up after himself so he held back and continued to eavesdrop. Nothing further was brought up and he felt himself drifting off to sleep. It wasn't until later that things heated up. He awoke to a morning confrontation between the two. He put Maya to the test and so far she was giving it her all but with no real progress. At first she asked nicely, then a bit more convincing and as a last resort she finally demanded the code outright. Peter would still not oblige to her request and insisted on asking her the reason behind it. Satisfied that she held tight to their exchange and the promise to her family's safety provided somewhat of comfort to the doctor. Seeing she was hitting a wall with her boyfriend infuriated her to the point where obscenities were used to get her point across. All this and still Peter did not budge. He wanted to barge into the room and demand the code himself, which he knew would be pointless. None of the other board members knew that his youngest scientist could hold up their ultimate plan, nor did he feel the need to tell them at this point. Sooner or later he would get what he was after. In the meantime, he had a ten o'clock Zoom call with all the leaders and dignitaries and then he had to once again terminate a large portion of civilization. He would program the database to decipher anyone over the age of sixty and the elimination would be put in place. This was to include the most important figure in the whole of the United States of America. Upon completing this age group, would guarantee the collapse of America. With no President in the White House, the country would dismantle.

58

Waking up in a cold sweat, Melanie sat up in her bed. Her nightshirt was drenched. She couldn't remember the last time she had an erotic dream. Images of the young captive Tommy wouldn't leave her mind. Add in the fact that she kept picturing him naked and her inner desires were stirred. Never had she ever felt this type of passion for an individual she briefly met. The touch of his hand sent some sort of sexual electrical current tingling throughout her body, and with the way that both of their eyes locked on one another, she was certain he felt something for her as well. Her gut instinct told her so. Her father warned her to not attach herself to this group of individuals upon their arrival. It was when her father first saw them brought into the bunker that he immediately knew they were trouble. Knowing she was their only child and world to them both, when Doctor Anglim asked for her to assist, an immediate red flag went up. From that moment she was told time after time to just do her job and keep her distance. Assuring them that was her only intention, she never thought her feelings would come into play. Something told her that whatever it took to safely protect this individual was worth the risk. This eased her mind. After cooling down and deciding to change her nightwear, she got up from bed and walked over to her dresser. Melanie changed out of the damp top and pulled on a dry one. She then went to the bathroom and returned to bed. She hoped and longed that sleep would fast approach. Instead, she was wide awake and kept picturing the good looking young guy named Tommy. It was in that moment she promised herself that she would never let anything happen to him. So much so that if push came to shove, a whole lot of people would be falling down, leaving her and Tommy standing tall and untouched.

59

Peter didn't have a second to think or even give chase to Maya before the door was pushed wide open. The moment she left the suite, four soldiers came rushing in and apprehended him. They took him by force and escorted him to an area of the bunker he hadn't seen before. They shoved him in a cell the size of a closet and locked it behind him. Walking out of the area, they closed the lights leaving him alone in the dark with only his thoughts to consider. Why would Maya press the issue to give her his entrusted configuration he took months to devise? What exactly happened when the young girl came and took her away? What was exchanged between Doctor Anglim and Maya that put pure fear into her? It all happened so fast, and then they were given the suite and treated like a king and queen. It was all falling into place now. The mad doctor must have threatened Maya to make her act the way she did, but with what such threats, he couldn't put his finger on. Something so drastic that Maya would resort to such measures and treat him like a stranger. Many ideas crossed his mind as he stood in a confined space in the pitch black. He needed to get the Doctor to hand over the vaccine that could save millions of lives. In return, he might have to offer up the code he calculated. Peter was very unsure if that was such a smart move. The doctor couldn't be trusted and there was no guarantee his life would be spared upon doing so. He needed to brainstorm the ideal plan of action that could ensure all of their safety. His head was pounding and he knew the start of an intense headache would soon follow. Racking his brain was taxing and he still hadn't come up with the perfect escape. At this stage of the game nothing was even close to perfect which worried him even more.

60

Dr. Anglim summoned his most trusted guard, Tim, and filled him in on what would take place with Peter in the next hour. He instructed him to make sure he was handcuffed and brought to the computer lab at precisely eleven forty five. He told Tim that he was to be left alone with Peter but to make sure there were a sufficient amount of guards standing outside the room in case things should get out of hand. He asked Tim to stay the closest, knowing his tactic to danger switched him to high gear in seconds, unaware to the notion that the danger was soon to be his own.

61

"Get your fucking hands off of me. I'm sick and tired of you assholes treating us like we're criminals. I've done nothing wrong. Open your fucking eyes and read the writing on the walls. We're all dead in the long run. Do you think after this whole plan of the doctor's that you guys will be left to live? You're all in for a major surprise." Rough handled in a way totally out of control, the guards led Peter to the computer lab where he was greeted by a smiling ex- employer and teacher. Trying desperately not to make eye contact with this deranged individual was useless. Every which way he shifted his eyes the doctor followed his gaze. The whole time they pushed him along to where he needed to sit, the doctor made sure to stare him down. Finally, when they sat him down in the chair across from the doctor, he managed to avoid his glances. He needed to break the tension forming just from locking eyes. He desperately looked for anything to distract him. Now, looking down at the bright white floor tiles was when the idea hit him.

Thinking back to what he just screamed at the guards about none of them surviving this ordeal gave him what needed to be done. Having regained his confidence, he decided to give it his best attempt at getting out of the bunker alive. Peter raised his eyes and was once again locked into a staring contest. He gladly accepted the challenge as he thought to himself 'bring it on.'

62

"Just how did we end up like this? You had so much potential and I was more than willing to teach you everything. And for what? A group of pathetic people who will die regardless." Doctor Anglim shook his head in disarray. "But no, you wanted to be the martyr and save the world. So much for that." Peter stirred in his chair. Having been handcuffed the moment he was taken from the cell left him defenseless. All he could do was sit there and listen. Noticing the clock on the far wall of the large room caught his attention. In just five more minutes more lives would be sacrificed for no known reason other than the sick mind of this man who sat across from him. Watching where Peter's eyes just went, the doctor took glory in what he stated next. "That's right my son. No, I take that back. At one point I might have considered our relationship to be more like father and son, but not now. You are worthy of nothing. My whole purpose in having you brought to me was to witness another of my glorifying moments. Look closely and feel free to roam around the lab watching each and every monitor. What you're about to see is another mass destruction compliments of me. Eliminate the weak and useless and leave only the strong and powerful. As simple as that."

"Really? As simple as that. Just push a button and boom! Kill millions and millions of innocent lives. You're sick! You know that. SICK!"

"Call it what you may, but brace yourself." Doctor Anglim started to type at a ferocious speed with only a minute to spare before hitting the final key to cause the destruction he so desired. After his morning Zoom call with all the other powerful people on board, he increased his age gap to stop at sixty years of age. The range was more than what he was willing to share during the call. It was part of the agreement that every age elimination was to be discussed in order to have every country prepared for the impact it would cause. Taking this next step may cause consequences he wasn't quite prepared for, but either way it needed to be done. Doctor Anglim wanted to rid the country of the most powerful person other than himself. President Neubert would never finish his term, as his termination was just seconds away.

63

Peter rose from his seat in total disbelief. All around him complete chaos took place once again worldwide. Globally, he watched as planes, trains and automobiles exploded, crashed and derailed all over the world. Turning away from all the madness left him weak in the knees and sick to his stomach. Mayhem reigned throughout the planet. No longer would any single place in this world function like it once did before the Rapid X Virus and now the mad doctor. Peter shuffled along a row of monitors. He was in search of any type of intercom button to activate without alerting the doctor. If he could get the doctor to open up to him about his ultimate and final plan, just maybe it would be in his favor. Desperately he continued to look at each station while avoiding the monitors with all the death and destruction. Doctor Anglim noticed Peter prancing around the room, and he decided to follow and probe him with more death on the screens. Doctor Anglim slowly made his way towards him. As he followed Peter, he couldn't help but to keep looking at the different monitors. Peter circled around the doctor while never once stopping what he intended to do once he found the button for the PA system. Sweat had broken out on his forehead and dampened his armpits. He silently prayed for a miracle. As luck would have it and as an answer to his prays, the switch for the entire complex was duly noted on the main phone of the doctor's desk. With his hands behind his back, he lifted them and pressed the button labelled PA. The doctor didn't notice him do this. By nothing short of a true miracle, the doctor was preoccupied with one of the many screens and missed Peter's actions, and in just a short time when being questioned, his whole plan was about to unravel.

64

President Neubert was fairly confident that sooner rather than later this would all come to an end. A peaceful one at best. He had called an urgent gathering of all his cabinet members. There were fifteen in total. Included were the Vice President, Amanda Caputo, as well as the Speaker of the House of Representatives, President of the Pro Tempore of the Senate, Secretary of State, Secretary of Treasury, Secretary of Defense, Attorney General, and seven other cabinet secretaries of various groups. Sitting in a circle in his Oval office, each of them listened and took notes as to the newest agenda issued from the Commander in Chief. Determined to overcome this deadly obstacle was their number one priority. Focused entirely on the situation at hand, each member nervously tried to suppress his or her inner anxiety. Watching the clock approach noon had eight of the people in the room scared senseless. Most of them were in their sixties and two were in their early seventies. As of yesterday, anyone seventy-five and over had died. All around the world this age group simply perished with or without any known medical history. President Neubert didn't feel threatened as he was promised by his close friend and confidant, Doctor Anglim, that he was given a vaccine that would evade his age group's demise. Having not shared this information so as to put him in the elite group over the others in his cabinet, left him guilt ridden. He was raised by devout Roman Catholic parents and was taught that to lie was an eternal sin. In this such case, he was left with no other choice. As if they were counting down a New Year's Eve celebration with resolutions to be kept, they were a mere ten seconds left to doomsday instead. Hoping and praying the outcome would be of just a few short years instead of a larger spread, had them all on edge. Perspiration could be seen on the foreheads of most. The clock on the wall as well as some of their apple watches struck noon. President Neubert stood from his chair feeling confident he was safe. A handshake by Doctor Anglim with a promise was enough to keep him calm. He rose rather fast to his feet, only to drop to the floor immediately. Seven others toppled off their chairs and hit the floor hard. The remaining seven, all under sixty, sat there in complete shock.

It wasn't until Vice President Caputo broke the silence with the most terrifying scream possible.

65

Completely satisfied with the President taken out of the equation and knowing the United States would crumble left the doctor with a gleaming smile upon his face. Distracted for the moment, he failed to see the PA system turned on as he taunted Peter. "Poor, poor pitiful Peter. You pathetic little fool. You could have risen to the top but you chose to try to be the savior. Tsk, tsk, shame, shame. I took you under my wings and taught you how to fly but you chose to fly the coop instead, taking with you a code that only you can decipher. Must I pull up the screen with all your family members to prove a point? I'm in such a good mood, I feel like I should continue this high. What do you think?"

"What do I think? Really, is that what you want to know?" Peter stood closer to what he hoped were microphones sending out their conversation throughout the entire bunker for all to hear.

"I think you are a monster who needs to be stopped! And if for one second you think I'd give you the code to have you continue your madness, then you really are crazy. I'm baffled as to how you even came across that I created something that could save at least half of the world's population after the Rapid X virus and now you. It all makes sense to me now. You must have threatened Maya to help you get what you needed. She loves me too much that she ran from the suite once she realized your plan was crumbling. The pressure was too much for her and she couldn't press me any longer. Even that fell through. You really think you can continue this madness don't you?"

"Continue? Why I don't plan on stopping until only the superior are left. If you don't sacrifice your code, then I'll design another vaccine to wipe out who I couldn't get to this first time around. It may take me some time but the world isn't rebounding any time soon."

"So that's what you intend to do, do you? Only the superior? What about all these so called workers of yours down here in this bunker? What's in it for them?" Peter held his breath as he baited the doctor for his final kill over the PA system.

"These people mean NOTHING to me! Just measly little pawns in the game of life. Don't you see Peter, I'm like that song...'I have the WHOLE WORLD IN MY HANDS.' I haven't decided how many of them I'll let live, but trust me if anything I can count on two hands how many. Perhaps I'll resort to an eeny meeny miny moe just to have some extra fun."

"Is that so? You have over five hundred employees working for you round the clock down here, and you will only offer life to no more than TEN!" Peter raised his voice as he mentioned the magically low number of ten or less.

"Seems unjust doesn't it? But there is no room in my new race for mediocre people of lower standards to join the newly elite. Sorry to say Peter, but it is what it is. I have it all planned. The Hoover Dam is two miles north of this bunker. I had the bunker built on lower grounds and directly in the path of the dam should it ever bust. I couldn't or should I say I wouldn't have the heart to punch in their ages individually to kill them off one by one." Laughing in a maniacal voice he continued, "I'd simply rather open the floodgates and let them all drown like the rats they are. Poor little creatures won't stand a chance as the flood waters rush in to the bunker and drown them all. They won't have time to catch their last breath yet alone try to escape."

"What makes you think you can be GOD? What gives you that right? Slaughtering innocent lives by the millions."

"God? Oh Peter, Petey, Pietro. Such silliness sputtered from your mouth. I'm better than God. God has already pre-planned deaths from each person the moment they were born. At different times and all random ages mixed. I, on the other hand, pre-determined each age group precisely the way I choose to. And yes, by the millions. After years and years of research and mostly by trial and error, I perfected it. I created a fool proof vaccination that I was able to insert a nano-chip the size of a piece of beach sand. Each chip contained every single human being in our worldwide census. I injected, as well as all the other countries around the globe, pertinent data for every single soul in the world, and by completing this I am able to punch in simple data that corresponds to every age available from infancy to over a hundred years or older. Of the seven billion worldwide people in the universe some did manage to avoid getting vaccinated. We have their names and information but as you can see we are a bit busy at the moment exterminating what we have."

"You do know you will rot in hell for this. Forgive me for even comparing you to God. You are the devil incarnate and surely the pits of hell are blazing with an eternal fire with your name on it."

"Is that so?"

"Trust me when I say you just buried yourself alive. You'll be burning rather quickly you twisted demented man."

Peter could no longer contain himself. He wanted to be the last one to get a word in as he explained what just took place with the PA system switched to the on position. Watching the color drain from the doctor's face was the satisfaction he had hoped for. Doctor Anglim quickly pushed past him and shut the PA off. Next he proceeded to lock the steel door leading into the computer lab, knowing fully well that an ambush would soon take place. How he had fallen for this was beyond him. There was no fixing what had just been said. He now feared for his life. As the steel door slowly continued to slide from left to right closing before what could be his ultimate death, his most trusted guard Tim was able squeeze in. Doctor Anglim nearly fainted when he saw that Tim no longer showed signs of respect, but rather more of a wrath looking to be unleashed.

66

Most employees were loyal people who sacrificed their whole lives for what they thought was the good of the cause. Promises were made that they now knew were false statements all along. Most of them stopped dead in their tracks shaking their heads in disbelief from what they were listening to. The silence was uncanny as you could hear a pin drop as soon as the PA system came on. The harsh reality of what followed from the doctor's conversation was unbelievable. Sacrificing THEIR lives after all they had done, only to be met with a horrible death. DROWNING! Slowly people started to mutter to one another what they planned to do next. Shuffling all around the bunker soon became complete chaos as employees didn't know whether to flee or seek revenge on this deranged man they no longer trusted.

67

"Is this for real? Are they just going to leave us here to die?" Tommy shouted at no one in particular. "What do you think is going to happen next? If I was out from these bars, I would track the doctor down and kill him myself." All ten of them listened to the intense conversation between Peter and the mad doctor. No one had been in to see them since the conversation ended and from what they could see, people were running in all different directions out in the hallway.

"Please Tommy, calm down! We need to think this through. No need to kill the doctor when apparently he holds the key to ALL our lives," Rita said with her motherly voice.

"Yeah bro, chill the fuck out!" Khang who barely ever spoke yet alone curse interjected.

"Khang, we don't speak to people like that. You know better than that," his sister Linh replied as she walked over to her brother to comfort him. "If we all start to snap and curse one another out then we are giving in to the madness. We need to work together to get out of this mess before it's too late," she continued.

"She's right! Let's all put our heads together and think this through. First off, we need to grab the attention of someone out in the hall and ask for their help," Karin suggested.

"And how do you suppose we do that? If you haven't noticed, it looks like sheer panic is in full form," Bill said after watching people run in every direction but theirs.

Nick, who had stayed silent longer than he should have spoke last. "Listen. Rather than bicker back and forth, I say we all put our voices together and scream out at the top of our lungs to grab someone's attention. Hopefully someone with compassion will stop and try to lend us a hand and if they can't, then just maybe they'll get someone who will." Absorbing what he just suggested, they all headed straight for the cell's bars and placed their faces in between them. With Nick now in charge and telling them on the count of three what needed to be done, the other nine eagerly awaited to shout like they never shouted before.

68

Melanie frantically searched in vain for her parents as total panic ensued in the hallways throughout the entire bunker. Pushing her way past many frantic employees, some who were her friends, felt endless. People were rushing past her and some even resorted to pushing her out of the way. She lost her balance twice and regained it before falling to the ground with the possibility of being trampled. After a few minutes, but what felt like an eternity, she found her parents in their living quarters. Her father was seated and pulling on his boots. Relief washed over both of her parents as their daughter entered the room. After rehashing what they all had heard and not knowing what exactly would take place next, they all agreed on what needed to be done. If her father remembered correctly the alarms and warning lights flashing and what they entailed, the Hoover Dam would play an integral part in their demise. Melanie would get the keys for the cell and release the people, one who she had strong feelings for, and her parents would go to the main level garage. They would try and rustle up two high terrain vehicles to get them far away from the bunker and to higher grounds. Unsure of the uncertainty of the doctor who they now knew was mad, left them with no other choice. With quick hugs and kisses the three of them said their goodbyes. They made a promise to meet up shortly in hopes to escape before it was too late, for both of them, unfortunately there would be no escaping.

69

"Listen Tim, you have it all wrong. I would never harm all of you. I knew he hit the button and I was playing along. You HAVE to believe me."

"I don't have to believe anything you say. Didn't sound like a joke to me. And if it was, why seal the door to this room?" Tim questioned the doctor as he slowly approached him. Peter, who was still handcuffed, listening to the conversation unfold and he knew he needed to act fast. Tim, at 6'5" and built like a defense player for the NFL, wasn't being so easily fooled a second time around. Peter decided to block him and pleaded, "Please, take these cuffs off of me. I need to get to my family before it's too late."

Tim snapped out of his trance and reached into his pockets and pulled out the keyring.

Fumbling with the ring, he finally found the key he was after. Peter backed up into him allowing easier access to release the cuffs. Once the cuffs were removed, Peter rubbed his wrists. They were red and had indentations from being put on so tight. While this was all taking place, Walter, going unnoticed reached down to the bottom drawer of his desk and pulled out a gun he had hoped to never have to use. Unfortunately as he watched the cuffs release from Peter's wrists, he raised the weapon and with his finger on the trigger waved it at the two terrified figures now stopped dead in their tracks.

"Don't make me pull the trigger. So help me God I'll do it! All I wanted to do was start the world over. Like hitting a reset button. With only perfect specimens of humans. I have to complete this task and NO ONE will stop me!" Peter stood still afraid to breath, yet alone move. Tim knew either way he was a dead man and bolted straight at the doctor, grabbing him by the waist. Doctor Anglim was caught off guard and was barely able to keep his grip on the gun. A struggle pursued as each man tried in vain to take control of the weapon. Staggering on their feet and swaying in every direction, a single shot was fired between the two bodies. Peter was still frozen in place and waited with bated breath to watch the doctor fall to the ground. What felt like an eternity but was only seconds finally came to an end as Tim turned to face Peter. Instead of a look of triumph, Tim held his stomach as blood poured endlessly from the bullet wound to his gut. Knowing he gave it his best attempt to stop the madness brought a smile to his face, even as his knees gave in and he fell to the floor to his untimely death.

70

Without an ounce of remorse for his dedicated deceased guard, Walter gained his composure and focused on the problem at hand. "Take one step in any direction and I'll shoot you between the eyes. With or without the fucking code. At this point now I could give two craps."

Standing in the same exact spot, Peter managed to muster up enough courage to speak after witnessing someone die feet away from him. "You'll never get away with this. You're a dead man too. Someone will get to you and give you the death you deserve."

The doctor sat down while keeping the weapon trained on Peter and started to busy himself on the keyboard. "You honestly think I wouldn't have back up plans in such emergencies as this. Granted I wasn't prepared for such a catastrophic delay, but there are always contingencies to dwarf them. You see Petey boy. I have my own helicopter above the bunker all set and ready for takeoff. All I need to do is grab my valise with the antidotes and off I go to my quiet resort built by me and for me and me ONLY, far in the northern regions of Napa Valley in Sunny California. I had every base covered and then some. Now all I need to finish up is to rid myself of every obstacle imaginable. Even if that means killing the dignitaries and world leaders that helped me get to this point. I need to start from scratch to tell you the truth. I broke my promise of killing the widest range from anyone sixty to seventy five which may have pissed a few off, so much so that they may send hitmen after me. Better to nip it in the bud before matters get out of hand. One tap of this button where I had all their chip ids stored and wham bam thank ya maam and poof, they're gone. As simple as that. Oh, and one last thing, by putting in the reverse code for the Hoover Dam, I just jammed the cylinders and the water is rapidly rising to a point where the walls won't be able to withstand the pressure and will outright burst. I give it five- ten minutes at most. Now if you'll excuse me, there isn't really all that much time and I truly don't have the heart to kill you. I honestly did think of you as my son. Wouldn't be nice to kill off another family member like I did my father. What kind of monster do you think I am?" He laughed out loud and continued, "But if you do try to follow me, I promise you I will shoot you straight through the heart."

71

The doctor slowly made his way across the wide room to the far wall where a keypad was present. While keeping one eye trained on Peter, with his other he hit several numbers on the pad and waited as a door slowly opened from the wall down. Carefully, he stepped through the door and once he was in a small hallway, he pressed a few more buttons to close it behind him. Leaving Peter behind and knowing his fate would take place underwater, he turned his back and hurried away as the door slowly started to close.

72

Peter watched the whole episode unfold in slow motion. His one-time mentor just made his escape to areas unbeknown to him. Snapping out of the trance that kept him frozen in place, he had mere seconds to decide his fate and the fate of his loved ones. Following the doctor might give him and the rest of the world a chance to survive. Deep down he knew the doctor would take all the vials that could vaccinate people with the life-saving antidote. Glancing to the exit out of the room and to his awaiting family saddened him. He knew that if God was on their side then the group would somehow manage to escape without him. His father and brother and even Bill would see to that. His gut told him so. The door where his now hated mentor just went through was almost closed. There was no more than eighteen inches to go before his only chance to save the universe still had hope. Peter made a mad dash and threw his body under the closing door with barely enough room to fit. If he had even waited another two seconds, his body would have gotten stuck and the door would have crushed him. Pulling himself up from the ground and brushing himself off, Peter went in the direction of the footsteps that echoed in the hallway.

73

Melanie rushed past people that were frantically trying to make their escape from the soon to be underwater tomb. Madness ensued and she was getting knocked in every direction. Several people she had known for years were pleading with her to go with them for her guaranteed safety. Ignoring their pleas and fighting the crowd going in the opposite direction, she finally caught a glimpse of the hallway that led to the cell that held ten innocent lives that needed rescuing. Pushing aside a guard who seemed to be going in there as well, she asked him what he intended to do. Walking aside one another at a faster pace than normal, he explained that he was instructed to finish off the group as soon as possible and in quick succession. With a rifle that she knew carried many rounds and with a gun attached to a holster on his waist, Melanie had to act fast. Agreeing that she, too, had been given special instructions to follow suit, she told the guard that in her haste to get there, she forgot her handgun. Assuming that what she said was the truth, the unsuspecting guard stopped for a brief second and unsnapped his revolver and handed it to Melanie. He quickly approached the cell where most of the group were still calling out for help from between the bars. As he readied himself to pull the trigger on any target within his range, he was taken aback when a sudden burst of gunfire hit him from behind, Staggering from the direct hit to his spine and knowing that death was imminent from the close proximity of the impact, he was able to pull off one single shot from his rifle.

Wobbling from side to side before collapsing, he turned to see who had rendered the final bullet to end his life. Surprised, stunned, and shocked were his final thoughts as he realized that he handed over his weapon to someone he thought was his ally but instead was his enemy.

74

Bill was the first to notice the two armed people running toward their direction. Before he even had a chance to warn the group two gunshots went off one right after the other. Screams were shouted as the man in front of the younger woman stumbled and fell to the ground lifeless. The younger woman who had visited them prior looked visibly shaken as she ran past the dead man and over to them. Fumbling with a set of keys and trying to insert one into the lock that held them prisoners, her hands shook uncontrollably. Bill and Nick stood at the entrance and watched as she finally opened the lock to offer them their freedom. When Rita let out a piercing scream, they both turned their heads in unison to what they never expected to see. One of their group took a fatal bullet to the chest and was bleeding out. She grabbed her chest and fell backward to the floor, not knowing exactly what happened and why she was the one whose luck just ran out.

75

Myleka dropped to her knees and took her mother's hand in her own yelling, "Momma, momma! Please momma don't die! Pleeasse…" Rita dropped down alongside Myleka while the others stood motionless watching the scene unfold. "Laureen, hold on! Do you hear me? Stay with us! Karin do something! You're the nurse!" She grabbed hold of a blanket nearby and placed the blanket over the wound on Laureen's chest trying to apply pressure to stop the bleeding. Karin, upon hearing her name called, dropped down on Laureen's other side and put her hand on the blanket as well. Linh and her brother stepped aside, crying while they did so. Laureen gasped for breath as her lungs were filling up with blood. Coughing up some blood, she managed to utter her last words, "Rita…Promise…me….you'll look after…my baby…girl… Promise me…" Struggling to catch her breath and gasping for air with whatever life she had left, Laureen reached out and took Myleka's hand, "Baby girl… momma loves you… larger than LIFE…remember that…

always remember…" Laureen exhaled and blood spewed from her mouth before she was able to finish her last few words. Her whole life flashed before her eyes and in a split second it was coming to an end. Thoughts and images of her and her daughter over the years went by in a blink. The last image was of her yelling out to people running past their cell and then an intense pain she never experienced, followed by a wetness spread across her chest. It all happened so fast that she didn't have time to absorb what actually occurred. There was a loud blast like the sound of a gunshot and then a severe burning sensation in her upper body. It hurt so much she willed it to go away and prayed the pressure would ease up. Unfortunately, her body had other plans for her and she spasmed once and then went still.

Myleka went hysterical, clutching on tighter and it took both Tommy and Maya to pull her off of her mother as she threw her body on top of her sobbing. Rita kept mumbling to herself, "I promise Laureen. I swear before God, I promise." Everything had spun out of control in a matter of seconds and when they all heard Melanie yell that they needed to leave right now, every one of them listened to what she said next.

76

Melanie had never fired a gun yet alone killed a person in the process. The guilt alone weighed heavily upon her. Never did she think she would be able to take another person's life. Knowing what his intentions were and with no time to evaluate the situation, she resorted to what needed to be done to save these innocent people from their certain deaths. She had to pull herself together in order to rescue this bunch of people, one of which she fell instantly in love with. After opening the cell door, she watched the horror unfold before her eyes. The youngest of the group was crying, screaming, and begging for her mother to wake up. Tommy, who she loved for reasons she couldn't quite explain, and Maya were trying in vain to lift the young girl off her dead mother. Total chaos was taking place and Melanie needed to put a stop to the madness if they were going to escape and survive before the floodwaters drowned them. In her bravest voice, she demanded all their attention. "Listen up! PLEASE, we don't have much time. Those alarms and the flashing red lights are indications that the Hoover Dam has been compromised. My father was briefed on these warning signs from Dr. Anglim on several occasions and trust me, we don't have much time. Apparently others must know the outcome too as total panic is in full pursuit. I know this is rather difficult, especially with the loss of one of your own, but if we don't LEAVE RIGHT NOW consider us all DEAD!" As if they were all broken from a trance, they followed her as she ran at full speed out of what was once their death trap and into the unknown.

77

Rita, whose hands were covered in Laureen's blood, took hold of Myleka and ushered her along. Myleka kept glancing over her shoulder to get one last glimpse of the mother she loved with all her heart and whom she would never hug or kiss again. Karin stood on the other side of her and tried to distract Myleka to no avail. Nick and Bill, visibly shaken as well, each took one of the sister and brother's hands and hurried them along. Tommy somehow managed to grab hold of Melanie's hand and kept pace with her. For the two of them it felt like the most natural thing to do, as if they had been lovers for years. Maya was the last of the group to follow along as she hoped and prayed she would get to ask for forgiveness for trying to betray the man she truly loved.

78

Melanie made her way through the maze of fellow employees hoping the group could keep up. With Tommy running alongside her, she felt more confident than imaginable, as if they alone could take on the world. With an occasional twist of her head to make certain the rest of the group followed, they were just a few hundred yards from the meeting place she had agreed to with her parents. They were to meet her in the garage on the main level of the bunker. Her father had access to most vehicles as he was also a trained mechanic who was utilized frequently to keep the fleet up to par. Melanie beelined to the staircase rather than the elevators for fear that the power may go out and they would be trapped inside one. With eight flights ahead of them, Melanie took a deep breath, opened the heavy metal door, and made a run for her life with all the others in tow.

79

Walter was determined to execute his final plan even if loyal lives were lost in the process. Sensing that everything he had worked to perfection was falling apart, and given what had transpired in the last couple of days made him resort to other more drastic measures. Now, with the release of the Hoover Dam, he resorted to his ultimate conclusion. Having gotten his pilot's license years ago to fly a helicopter, he purchased a Military Sikorsky UH-60 Black Hawk and kept it fully fueled and on the rooftop of the bunker. The cost alone was over twenty million dollars and to be trained to operate it cost him another two million out of pocket. The financial support from his investors in other countries with the promise of surviving eased the expenses. In such emergencies, Doctor Anglim had easy access to the chopper and knew that this was his best escape route. It could reach a top speed of 222mph. The length of the helicopter was sixty-five feet long and was stocked with supplies that could sustain him up to a year. He also wanted to take his top ten employees with him but with all that transpired it was useless at this point. Within minutes, a wall of water would come cascading down and completely cover the bunker, flooding it within seconds. Not a living soul would be able to survive unless they reached higher grounds. At the rate and speed of the water, they would have to act fast, and time was not in their favor. Either way, Walter couldn't care less. In a few short hours he would be nestled away in his hideaway and the next phase of his plan of action would be put in place. But as of right now, he needed to focus on the matter at hand. He needed to secure the vials of the antidote that could save millions of lives, lives he didn't really care to save. He created the antidote regardless, just in case he needed to prove he was working diligently to save humanity. Walter had placed the Stealth Black Extra-Large Anvil Attache near the exit closest to the helicopter pad landing. Now, as he opened the cabinet that held the case he smiled to himself, satisfied that the end was near. Whose end was soon to be determined.

80

Peter had to slow down in order to listen to which direction the footsteps were headed. The echo off the hollow walls made it difficult to distinguish which way the doctor was going. There were so many hallways jutting in all different directions that Peter felt like he was in a maze at a carnival. Concentrating the best he could, he would periodically stop and listen intently. Knowing he was losing ground on the doctor had him breaking out into a cold sweat. Deep down he knew he couldn't lose the doctor's trail. If he did, he and his family would most certainly die. Taking a deep breath, he took the path he prayed was the right one. If it wasn't, all the prayers in the world couldn't save him.

81

Walter pushed through the metal exit door which led to the landing pad. With the attache case firmly in hand, he swiftly moved to the helicopter and to his presumed safety net. He placed the case in the seat beside where he would be flying and lifted his leg to get inside. Once he fastened his seatbelt, he took all the necessary precautions, and soon after the blades started to circulate. It was at that precise moment that out of the corner of his eye he saw movement. Fast approaching was the last person he had hoped to ever lay eyes on again. Running at full speed and with pure hatred in his eyes, it was none other than Peter, the person he now hated the most in this world.

82

Walter put the lever in gear and the helicopter proceeded to slowly lift off the ground. He started to push the button needed to increase the swirl of the blades to fly higher faster. With one eye permanently fixated on Peter and the other on the controls, Doctor Anglim hoped for the best and feared for the worst. Taking his eyes off of Peter to try to get better access to the control panel was the wrong decision to make. With the helicopter no more than two feet off the ground, there was a sudden jolt to one side of the craft. Looking over his shoulder, Walter cursed out loud. Hanging on the lower blade of the chopper was his nemesis.

83

Peter held on tightly for dear life. As luck would have it, he had chosen the correct path. Off in the distance he heard the evil doctor slam shut a cabinet door again, confirming he was heading in the right direction. As he got closer, he caught a glimpse of the doctor holding a rather large black case, which he was certain was the life-saving vials, and he watched as he made a mad dash for the exit. Peter had no time to waste and quickly picked up his pace. Remembering that the doctor still had the gun didn't prevent him from slowing down. He pushed aside that thought and continued until he reached the door and forcefully opened it, just as Doctor Anglim had moments ago. Seeing that the helicopter was leaving the ground, Peter didn't hesitate for even a split second. If he waited a second longer, any attempt to get on board would prove futile. As Peter ran at top speed, he mustered up all his courage and leapt in the air and made contact. Trying desperately to swing his legs and make contact to gain access into the helicopter was exhausting his efforts. If he didn't get into the craft, he was certain he would fall to his death, a death he never imagined quite like this.

84

The sound of all their footsteps rushing up the stairs was deafening to their ears. Regardless, this didn't slow them down as they continued their journey to safety.

Tommy let go of Melanie's hand and opened the door to the parking garage. He, too, felt feelings for this young woman who he had only met a short while ago. Taking on the role of protector, he ushered past her and slowly pushed the door open. Total chaos was taking place in the garage as many employees, along with their own families, searched for a vehicle to escape before the flood. Word spread fast of the dam being released or destroyed depending on what was passed along to them. People were running amok to find a means of transportation to get away fast. Tommy and Melanie were the first to join the confusion surrounding the whole lot. The others followed suit and now they were all huddled in a small circle, astonished at the madness unfolding right before their eyes. Melanie was trying desperately to stay calm as she scanned the lot looking for her parents who promised to be there first. With the large amount of people running, pushing, and frantically in pursuit of their own transportation, it made it near impossible for her to spot them. With help from Tommy, she stood atop the nearest car's roof and looked in every possible direction to locate her parents. From afar, she saw her father jumping up and down waving an article of some type of clothing. Jumping down from the car's hood, she turned to the group and told them to stay close behind her as she ventured into the madness. Amidst the turmoil, twice the group was nearly separated and only managed to stay together due to the diligence of Nick and Bill. Both men used their strength to herd the group along and usher them to the awaiting vehicles. After what felt like a lifetime, but was only a minute or two at most, they were united with Melanie's parents. Quick hugs and fast acknowledgments were made, and the group, which now consisted of twelve, needed to split up. Melanie's dad, who had to draw a weapon on fellow employees he had worked with for years, looked visibly shaken in the process of keeping access to the two high terrain Jeeps he had keys for. Twice he threatened two men to stay clear of the Jeeps and during one confrontation, he nearly pointed the loaded handgun at the chest of a determined man who also had a family he wanted to protect. Waving the loaded gun with his finger on the trigger showed the man that Melanie's father meant business and the man ran off. All around them, people jumped into other vehicles and sped off. With no time to spare, Nick and Melanie's father decided on who would ride with who. Melanie was very familiar with the territory outside the bunker as she and her father often made trips back and forth to the dam at the Doctor's instructions. She would drive one of the six passenger Jeep Wrangler Rubicons. Tommy, along with Maya, Linh, Khang, Rita and Myleka would just fit. Rita needed to be with them to comfort Myleka who moved about in a daze. Melanie's parents along with Nick, Bill and Karin would follow closely behind in the second Jeep. Safely secured in the Jeeps, Melanie drove to the exit from the garage as others were leaving in vehicles too. Some cars in haste winded up crashing into other vehicles causing a bit of a traffic jam. People who didn't manage to occupy a means of transportation for themselves were jumping onto the trunks of cars to get out before they drowned. Gunshots were heard all around the garage as people were desperate and knew their time was limited. No longer were they fellow employees who shared a common bond for Epigen Hyperspace as their friendly work environment. Now they were mere human beings in a fight for survival and only the fittest would win.

85

The two Jeeps pulled out and were now behind a slew of other vehicles. Melanie's dad briefly pulled alongside her and put down his passenger window where Nick was seated. They discussed the path that would lead them to higher grounds and ensure their safety. Melanie was just about to give the Jeep gas, when she heard a beep on the dashboard alerting her that the left passenger door had opened. Looking in her driver's mirror she couldn't believe what she saw. Maya was the one who had opened the door and quickly jumped out of the Jeep, and she was running back toward the bunker.

86

Maya couldn't believe her eyes. Worrying for the last hour as to where Peter could be, she left it up to faith that he would make his escape, too. Tommy, who also was concerned for his brother, convinced Maya that Peter would make it out one way or another. With all they had been through it was in God's hands whether they would live or die. Convinced that Tommy was right, she agreed with his sentiment. Just then, off in the distance as they stopped to confirm their getaway path, the sound of a helicopter could be heard. As Maya sat behind Melanie, who she now trusted fully, her instinct had her look one last time at the bunker from where the noise was coming from. When she looked up she nearly fainted. Running across the roof was Peter. It looked like he was heading in the direction of the helicopter. Without even thinking, she opened the door of the Jeep and jumped out. With shouts from both Jeeps to get back in, their voices went unnoticed. Maya needed to be with the only man that she ever loved. Avoiding rushing cars swerving around her, she ran to the side of the bunker to a fire escape that would take her to the roof and to the man she needed to forgive her. She was in fast pursuit to hold, hug, and kiss the man of her dreams. She wanted to be with Peter no matter what the price may be. Unbeknown to her, it was a hefty price that would be paid.

87

Tommy put his hand on the door handle and proceeded to open it. He was going to try and stop Maya from leaving the Jeep. Nick, his father, yelled for him to get back in. He would handle the situation. Bill, along with Nick, stepped out from their Jeep, while Melanie's father told her in a firm voice to speed away. He promised that they would be no longer than a few minutes at most lagging back. Tommy nodded and closed the door. Melanie, who did almost everything her parent's wanted her to, pressed down on the Jeep's gas pedal and left a spray of dust as it drove away.

88

Nick, knowing there wasn't much time to waste, ran after Maya as Bill trailed closely behind. He couldn't leave her as he considered her more like a daughter than just his son's girlfriend.

Peter, who he was very worried about, would make it out of the bunker. His fatherly instinct told him so. Maya was faster than he thought possible as she grabbed hold of the first rung on the fire escape and quickly climbed it. She was determined to get to the roof for reasons he didn't know. What he did know was that he was no longer twenty-five himself and climbing after her would prove useless. The floodwaters would be there momentarily and there were four other lives at stake other than his own. Leaving Maya at her own destiny was a difficult decision but one that had to be made. Turning around and grabbing Bill by the arm to head back to the Jeep, Nick made the sign of the cross and said a silent prayer.

89

The Hoover Dam created Lake Mead, the largest reservoir in the U.S. with a surface area of 247 square miles. The dam could store up to 9.2 trillion gallons of water from the Colorado River (nearly two years of its flow), if necessary. The maximum water pressure at the base of Hoover Dam was 45,000 pounds per square foot. Anything in its path would be completely demolished in seconds. The water level reached its max and with the aid of a built in explosive device that was automatically detonated with the assistance of a mad scientist, the floodgates were released and mass destruction along with the loss of many more lives was soon to follow.

90

Melanie focused on the open road before her. Having travelled it many times over, she knew exactly how to maneuver any obstacles that blocked their path. Glancing in her rear-view mirror hoping to spot her father's Jeep consumed her. Tommy was trying to make conversation but she blocked it out, not deliberately, as she heavily concentrated on the road while also checking her mirror for her parent's Jeep to appear. Other vehicles tried to keep up with her as they assumed she knew where she was headed, when in reality she had no idea.

91

Trees were swept away as if they were ice cream sticks tossed to the curb. Huge boulders were also carried along like they too, were pebbles being thrown to skip the top of the ocean. The raging water continued its unstoppable path as it cleared any object that it came in contact with. The bunker was in the exact direction it was making its way towards. There was no time for the remaining people to escape. If they hadn't drove off by now, they wouldn't make it to higher grounds. The water was at least a mile wide and forty feet in height. A tsunami of its own creation roared with a frightening sound. People stopped in their tracks when they first heard the noise, then they snapped out of it hoping they still had time, which unfortunately they didn't.

92

Melanie kept the speedometer to a safe speed as she continued to steer the Jeep to the highest spot she knew was around. It was at the sound of a noise one could never quite describe that made her pull over. All of the occupants of the Jeep except for Myleka stepped out. Rita as well as Tommy and Melanie looked back down the road they had just come from. Cars, trucks, and pickups all either sped past or pulled over near them. There was no sign of the other Jeep that contained their loved ones. No one needed to state the obvious dismal fate of the others. The water spread across the road about one hundred yards from where they parked as it still made its way downhill. There was no denying what they all surmised. No one uttered a word. As they stared at the rushing water from the broken dam, Rita was the first to break down and cry. Tommy rushed over to his mother with tears in his eyes and wrapped her in his arms to comfort. Linh and Khang also cried as they also felt a loss first of Laureen and now Bill who were both like family to them. Myleka somehow was fast asleep through the whole ordeal, either from total mental anguish or mere exhaustion from her mother's death. Melanie was the last to react. Tommy let go of his mother and quickly stepped toward her as she fainted, but instead of falling to the ground, she landed safely in his arms. The realization was too much for all of them and it would take a very long time for any of them to heal. For now, they were safe, and only time would tell for just how long.

93

The noise was deafening. Nick and Bill quickly jumped in the vehicle. Turning back as he stepped in, Nick saw a look of sheer panic in both Karin and Melanie's mother's eyes. Without uttering a sound, Melanie's father stepped on the gas and followed the direction his daughter went just a few minutes ago. Certain his daughter made it to the spot they had spoken about put his mind and heart at ease. Staring in the rear-view mirror his eyes locked on the only other person that he still loved more than life itself. About a dozen other packed vehicles all tried to head up the road. A few crashed into one another stopping them in their tracks and sealing their fate. Melanie's father swerved around them and was lucky to avoid other collisions by doing so. Each of the five watched as a huge wave tumbled over any object underneath it. The water was spreading from their left at an amazing speed. The Jeep was so close to safety, yet so far. The volume of the wave sent shivers through all their spines. Nick was the first to realize that they weren't going to make it. He took in a deep breath which he knew was pointless but for the moment felt necessary. Rita would take care of their boys and Maya, as well as the other three younger ones who would now need her more than ever. This brought much comfort to him knowing they would survive. Now, as much as the Jeep went over the rough terrain, it was useless. The dam's rushing water loomed over the vehicle so fast, it left them with no time to react. It was useless to continue but Melanie's father gave it his all. Her mother took hold of Karin's hand and squeezed it gently knowing what was to come. She also stared in the rear-view mirror and never took her eyes off her husband as tears now flowed from her as well. Tears streamed down Karin's cheeks as she openly prayed the 'Hail Mary' out loud. Bill, who made peace with himself at that precise moment, was the only one to smile, as he too, knew the others who he had grown to care very much for were going to live. The wave hit the jeep with such force that all the windows were smashed wide open. Bill was the first one swept out of the right rear passenger window. Melanie's mother's hand was pulled from Karin's grasp as she went out the back window of the Jeep with Karin right behind her, drowning them instantly. Melanie's father and Nick barely had a chance to do anything as they simultaneously were tossed out the front windshield and were dead before they knew it.

94

Maya was exhausted but never gave up as she finally made it to the rooftop. Pulling herself up, she stood and ran in the same direction Peter had. Calling out his name was useless. He was too far away to hear her and the noise from the rotors of the helicopter only made it more difficult. Besides, he appeared to have been about to make a mad leap to the helicopter that was slowly taking off from the landing pad. Maya, winded from the climb, sprinted to the pad. Peter, who had his back to her, fought to make his way up and into the helicopter. He dangled from the legs of the craft, the whole while attempting to get enough leverage to gain access into the chopper. He accomplished the task and pulled himself in using his stomach to wiggle aboard. As Maya was fast approaching the helicopter which still was within reach, she saw what appeared to be a tidal wave heading her way. Horrified and panic stricken, Maya knew she only had seconds before the water would cover the entire bunker and everything around it. Screaming and frantically waving her arms, Maya eventually managed to catch Peter's attention. "Oh God! Peter! HELP ME! Please help me!" Not believing his eyes as he saw the woman he loved most and knowing time was crucial, he yelled back, "Quick Maya! You got to run quicker! Hurry!"

"Oh God Peter! I'm trying. Please don't leave me here. PLEASE…"

The helicopter starting rising and in another moment the distance would be too high for her to reach him. "You gotta trust me babe! Just run and JUMP! Don't even think about hesitating. Got it?"

Maya, with fear sketched across her face, didn't give it a second thought as she was inches away from the edge with Peter hanging down with his hands out. She leapt full body into the air and over the side of the bunker with her arms outstretched. With her eyes closed, she prayed her hands would lock with Peter's, and by a miracle they did. He caught her by her wrists, and swinging back and forth like a pendulum she kept repeating what her intentions were. "Peter, I'm so sorry. So sorry! Please don't let me go."

"I got you babe! Just hold on!"

"I'm trying. Please lift me in. I'm so scared!"

The helicopter swayed to the left as the weight heavily dipped to that side. Between the doctor and now the two of them, it was dangerously close to spinning out of control. If the chopper did indeed lose its course, the whole of civilization would be lost.

95

Walter cursed out loud. He could not even begin to process just how fast his luck had changed. As he boarded the craft, his future looked brighter than ever. He would be the sole survivor of the plan he took years to create. He would ensure that his allies were destroyed and if they weren't, he would take care of them himself. He smiled thinking about how the once trusted leader of Italy, Christopher Zappia, would try in vain to put the Malocchia or evil eye on him. The Malocchia-also called the Maloik, or evil eye-is an Italian curse, according to superstition. As President Zappia felt the instant pain of imbedding death, he would know that he was double-crossed, and he would try desperately to cast the spell, but he wouldn't have time. For a brief second, Walter had second thoughts and then pushed them out of his head. He would lay low and continue to wipe out age groups as he so desired until no human being existed. Then he would slowly rebuild the world as he wished, but before that could even happen, he had a constant thorn in his side that needed to be removed once and for all. Just how Peter managed to follow him out of the bunker and now into the helicopter baffled him. He needed to rid himself of Peter once and for all. Trying to steady the chopper which pulled to his left was getting more difficult. He thought he had leveled the craft with Peter when he spotted the girl whose named slipped his mind. She jumped from the ledge and now hung from Peter's hands. The helicopter jolted so fast to the left that the gun he had on his lap went flying into the air and right out the open door. Walter was weaponless and again couldn't believe his bad luck continued. Trying to upright the chopper before they all went into the raging water just a few yards away, he threw the lever straight up. The helicopter jolted and rose so fast that Walter was thankful he was strapped in. He also hoped that from the sudden jolt, the two pesky pests would fall to their deaths.

96

Peter had just shimmied his body up and into the helicopter. He couldn't believe he managed to do so. At this point he had no plan in mind as to how to stop the doctor. He knew Walter had the gun still on him, and Peter needed to proceed with caution or likely take an unwanted bullet. As he was just about to push up off the floor, he caught an image that couldn't be possible. His one and only true love, Maya, was running and shouting toward him. He could barely make out what she was saying and put together bits and pieces that made sense. She was apologizing for what he assumed was her betrayal. He was never mad at her and knew that she was pressured and threatened into it by the insane doctor. She also pleaded with him to get her onboard the craft. He told her to trust him and take the leap which she blindly did. Now, as the helicopter rose high enough to miss the surging tsunami that slammed into the bunker eradicating all, Peter felt his grip loosening on Maya's wrists. Swerving so fast to gain speed and level the aircraft caught Peter off guard. He was lifting Maya with every ounce of strength he had left. Perspiration dripped from his forehead and into his eyes in the short time he held onto her wrists. He looked down at Maya as she now had her eyes wide open with pure fear etched in them, "Oh GOD! I feel my hands slipping…My HANDS are slipping Peter. OH GOD…" With every ounce of energy Peter had left, he tried to pull her up all the while praying he wouldn't let go.

97

Maya closed her eyes and jumped. When her wrists were caught by Peter, she thanked God. For someone not truly spiritual, God was on her side. She felt Peter pulling her up and finally opened them. Peter was staring into hers with glimmers of hope as he used all his upper body strength to get her onboard. She knew she was just a foot or so away from making it on. Then a sudden jolt sent the chopper soaring straight up. The doctor must have lifted the level faster than anticipated to avoid the onslaught of deadly waters fast approaching. By doing so, the huge tidal wave just missed the helicopter. It slammed into the bunker and washed away anything in its path which included cars filled with people and people scrambling around on the ground outside. Thankfully so, every one of those innocent lives were swept away without a moment to know what hit them.

98

The sudden thrust of the chopper to the straightened position loosened their grip on one another. As Peter fiercely held her wrists and she her hands around them, the shift in the craft dangerously impacted their efforts. Maya's one hand slipped from Peter's grasp. Now dangling above rushing currents of certain death, Maya felt the need to say what her heart truly felt. After first pleading to save her and realizing it wasn't going to be possible without her taking Peter with her, she knew he needed to live to save what was left of humanity. As these last thoughts crossed her mind and she faced the inevitable, she took a totally different approach as petrified as she was. She would place her faith in God and if she somehow was meant to live, which was most likely not going to be the case, then she wished for it to happen fast and be painless. Having saved her family in the process of almost betraying Peter, she yelled above the noise as best she could, "Peter, let me go! You'll fall to your certain death with me...YOU have to let me go! Always remember that I LOVE you and always did!"

Peter couldn't fathom what she was saying. He would never let her go regardless of her pleading at this precise moment. With sweat dripping off his face and blurring his vision, he tried in vain to hold her one hand. His armpit felt like it was ripped from the socket but that didn't stop his endless effort to keep hold of her. He screamed down to her, "Never ever will I let go! DO you hear me! NEVER!...Just hold on...Please Maya! I need you and LOVE you more... Now hold on tight!"

Peter leaned out until he, himself, felt like he was going to fall. With a sudden burst of adrenaline, Peter yanked as hard as he could, feeling as if he just pulled her arm out of its socket as well. As if both of their prayers were answered, Maya was suddenly airborne and pulled directly into the craft and on top of him. Crying tears of relief and now momentous joy, he stood up and scooped her into his arms, kissing her entire face in the process. Maya was safely onboard and he would never, ever again let her go. Little did the two lovers know that it was out of their control what would happen next.

99

Walter watched the whole scene unfold before his own eyes. Having just saved his own life from the gigantic wave that just missed the helicopter, he turned his head to witness the unimaginable. Peter had somehow managed to pull Maya into the back of the helicopter. Safely in his arms and sobbing and returning his kisses, he knew what needed to be done and fast. With his right hand on the control lever, he swiftly moved it to the left again causing the craft to slant sideways enough to have the two lovers lose their balance, enough so that he knew that at least one, if not the two of them, were certain to lose their footing causing them to tumble out the side, with no time to react other than falling to their certain death.

100

Maya was returning the kisses in rapid succession all over Peter's face as he did the same. Once their lips met one another's, the passion was ignited and any prior unnecessary thoughts were pushed to the side. They released their arms that held one another and were touching each other's bodies all over. Maya placed both her hands on his cheeks and brushed them gently across. Maya knew his love for her was never-ending, much the same as hers was for him.

Repeating their 'I love you', back and forth to one another at least a half a dozen times each, they were unaware of the unexpected shake of the chopper to the left. With no time to steady themselves, Maya who had her back to the wide opening, felt herself falling backwards. She let go of his cheeks and tried to grab his hands that were holding her shoulders. What happened next, happened so fast. Maya wasn't able to grab hold of one of Peter's hands. The slant was too much and she couldn't gain her balance or footing.

Maya's final attempt was useless. She didn't even have time to utter any last words of her undying love to Peter. Instead, her body tumbled straight out of the helicopter and right into the waiting currents, with open arms, to wash her away for all of eternity.

101

Peter kept smothering her with kisses all the while telling her how much he, too, had loved her. With his hands on her shoulders as she caressed his cheeks, he knew their love was never- ending. Then out of nowhere, the helicopter tilted to the left so suddenly that they had no time to catch their balance. Moments ago, Maya was safely on board and in his arms, and in the blink of his eye, she was falling to her death in the rapids below. Peter felt himself going out the open door right after her and would have if his hand didn't catch hold of the cargo net on the inside wall. Peter didn't know what possessed him to stick his hand out or why he even bothered, but he did and it saved his life, a life with no purpose now. Then it hit him. This was no accident. The helicopter was deliberately shifted to make them fall out. Peter knew the culprit behind it and would make this man pay, but the image of Maya with her hands outstretched as her body hit the water took control of his whole entire being. At that precise moment all he could do was hold on for dear life the whole while screaming until his voice was hoarse, one word over and over again, "NO..."

102

"I'll kill you with my bare hands you BASTARD! You filthy, twisted, demented, evil BASTARD!" Peter was afraid to let go of the cargo net for fear of flying out of the aircraft himself. With both sides of the military helicopter wide open, keeping his balance was his main objective. Peter held onto the cargo net as he bounced around like a Raggedy Ann doll. Twice he dropped to his knees crying aloud for the loss of his future wife. Getting back on his feet and slowly making his way to the cockpit was all he hoped for. Putting his hands around the doctor's throat and tightening his grip was what he intended. However, the helicopter swayed from side to side making it near impossible to complete this task. Screaming out in frustration, he continued his trek.

103

Walter didn't feel a bit of remorse for Maya's death. He leaned out the side of the craft and watched as she reached out in a last minute desperate attempt to be saved, all in vain though as she plummeted into the waiting waters. Hearing Peter's cries and then his sudden threats snapped the doctor back to reality. Acting fast, he decided his best chance of survival was to sway the aircraft back and forth so Peter couldn't reach him. He knew he could never make the full journey to his hideaway. He now resorted to landing the chopper on the heliport that was still intact on a mostly demolished wall, the remaining wall of the Hoover Dam.

104

The Sikorsky military aircraft made a very bumpy landing on the pad. Peter, who was not wearing a seatbelt, was tossed to the floor of the chopper. This gave Walter time to unfasten his and jump out of the helicopter. Walter knew his time was limited and resorted to the best approach possible to save his life. With the attaché case in hand, he slowly backed away from his worst nemesis imaginable. Having lost the handgun, Dr. Anglim's only means for his survival was what he carried in the large briefcase. Convincing Peter to spare him his life was his only concern. Catching Peter off guard, a simple push off the dam would solve it all. Making sure he kept his own footing, Dr. Anglim retreated slowly toward the exit that would lead him to another high terrain vehicle he had hidden there. This vehicle was only to be used if all other efforts proved useless. On account that both of the doctor's plans of A & B had failed, he now relied on Plan C. If this plan also came to ruins, then all else was lost.

105

It took Peter a few moments to catch his bearings as the helicopter made such a harsh touchdown. He was thrown to the ground and almost lost consciousness. Scrambling to his feet as he lifted himself up with the aid of the cargo net that had saved his life, Peter slowly approached the exit. His body had taken a beating and his heart was broken but still he knew what had to be done. Watching the doctor walk backwards from him with the attaché case in hand, Peter mentally needed to come up with a quick plan. Millions of lives were at stake, and Peter would stop at nothing to save them.

106

"Stay clear of me you! Do you hear me? Don't make me throw this case over the edge. If you come any closer I will!"

The wind had picked up and the dam itself was utterly destroyed. There was only this one section remaining that provided them with safety. The current of the raging waters brushed against the wall and if it should collapse, the both of them would fall over seven hundred feet to their deaths. Peter had picked up his pace and was closing the gap between them. "How could YOU? What possessed you to do something like this? You're sick and you deserve to die. You killed millions, and you killed Maya, and now you WILL PAY!"

Walter took each step slowly, keeping his eyes fixed on Peter. "Is that what you think? Poor, poor ignorant Peter. All I wanted was to recreate the perfect world and you could have been an integral part of it, but you chose your girl over being part of the new elite world order."

Peter felt his blood boiling and tried to keep his composure as he gained ground. He devised a new idea that popped into his head. He wanted to trick the doctor into believing he was on his side. Once he had the doctor convinced, he would make his final move. "Why did you have to kill her? Maya? Why? We both could have joined you. You didn't give us the chance. Instead you caused her to fall to her death." Peter cringed as he spoke those last words.

The doctor was confused for a moment as to what he was hearing. Just seconds ago he was being threatened and now coaxed into what he was sure were lies. "Wasn't the life of one such as your beloved Maya worth the lives of millions? Look at it this way son, what I hold in my hand is much more valuable than one. Wouldn't you agree? And I do hope you would agree. It would be such a shame to toss this case into the abyss below. Then it would ALL be for nothing. Maya's life included."

Peter wanted to spit in his face for having the audacity to refer to him as his son. He felt steam stemming from his ears when he once again mentioned Maya's name and acted like her life was meaningless. He despised this man in so many ways. He was a few feet away from the doctor now. If he made a run at him, he could be on top of him in seconds, hopefully before the doctor could toss the case over the ledge and into the rising waters never to be seen again.

107

The dam's remaining wall was forced to take the full impact of the building water. The pressure was weighing heavily against the concrete and what was once a small dent in the fissure, was now spreading rapidly. As Peter was just about to bounce on the doctor, the wall shifted and a piece of the dam shook and then shattered. A large section of the wall came crumbling down and left both Peter and Walter alone on the damaged part. Peter fell from the impact and was caught off guard. Walter gauged the gap between the two remaining sections to be about a three to four foot jump. While Peter fumbled on the ground to regain his footing, Walter wasted no time. He quickly tossed the briefcase to the other side. It landed smack in the middle of the cement, unscathed. He had no other choice. His only option was to make the four foot leap safely to the other side. With bated breath, he made the quick leap.

Sailing mid-stride, he took in a lungful of air and held it in. Once his feet hit the ground, he put his hands on his knees and blew out his breath. He made it to safety. Now all he needed was to high tail it out of there, leaving Peter behind.

108

Peter was thrown to the ground when the dam shifted and crumbled. As he started to rise to his feet, he watched in horror as the doctor jumped across the large gap and landed safely on the other side. Peter was trapped. He had to move fast if he was going to retrieve the case. As the doctor turned to run back to the chopper, Peter ran full speed and with both legs splayed out in front of him, jumped. Peter went airborne and within what felt like forever, made an abrupt landing on the other side. He quickly got to his feet and started after the doctor. As he was an arms-length from grabbing hold of him, the dam shook once again. This time the force caused the doctor to lose his balance and tumble off the side, but not before grabbing hold of a piece of rock that stuck out from the wall. The attaché case fell from his hands and landed on its side away from the edge. Dangling high above the waters, he called out for Peter to help him. As his first attempts went unanswered, he resorted to pleading, followed by begging to be spared.

109

Peter was again thrown to the ground. As he laid there, he heard the doctor calling his name. Not realizing where he was at first, he didn't answer. After crawling to where the voice was coming from, he took notice of the doctor's hand hanging on to a rock jutted out from the wall. Shortly after, he heard more pleading to be helped and finally begging to be saved.

"Peter, you can't leave me like this! Please, you can't! After all I've done for YOU! You have to save me! Do you hear me? YOU HAVE TO!"

Peter was confused as to what he was hearing. He continued to crawl in the direction of the doctor for reasons unknown. He made his way to the edge and peered over. The doctor was barely holding on and fear was clearly written all across his face. Peter looked over his shoulder and saw the briefcase within his reach. Contemplating what he should do next left his head dizzy with uncertainty. Was he really capable to let the man who mentored him die such a cruel death even after all he had done to millions of innocent lives, including the one person he was meant to spend his life with but now would never get the chance. Knowing he should just grab the case and flee to safety to feeling the pull in his stomach telling him something different, Peter stopped dead in his tracks. Standing up, he proceeded to head towards the case then came to an abrupt halt. As much as he hated this man and wished him dead, he couldn't let him fall to his death. Even with the image of Maya reaching out for him to save her, he found himself turning his body around. Without pausing, Peter reached out his hand as he kneeled down. Doctor Anglim didn't waste a moment in grabbing onto Peter and their hands interlocked. With an adrenaline rush, Peter gave one hard swift tug and the doctor was easily pulled up and over the ledge where he rolled onto his back. Panting from exhaustion, Walter slowly regained his composure. Acting once again as the loathed individual he was, he reacted on his gut instinct. As Peter turned his back on Walter to retrieve the case, he felt two arms wrap themselves around him. "You really are quite the stupid fool Peter. Did you really think I would let you run off with my prized possession?"

"Let go of me! I should have let you DIE! What the fuck was I thinking? You cold-hearted bastard!"

"Again, you clearly weren't thinking and now you'll never be thinking again." Walter held tight as he used both of his feet to push Peter closer to the edge of the prism.

With Peter in such a tight grip, there was no way he could break free. Walter was just about to release his grasp and push Peter over, when once again the dam shook and a huge section broke loose. The movement of the concrete breaking apart caught both of them off guard. As the doctor lost his hold on Peter, Peter tumbled face forward and hit the pavement. Anglim lost his footing and couldn't regain it as he fell backwards and stumbled toward the edge. In a last ditch effort, the demented doctor made one final effort to save himself, but in the end it was useless. The doctor couldn't regain his stance and went sailing off the edge and straight into the depths of hell. Peter watched the whole thing unfold right before his eyes. This time he had no guilt in watching the doctor fall to his death. The nightmare was finally over, and a new day was dawning. Peter just hoped it wasn't too late. He quickly grabbed hold of the attaché that contained what would save the rest of civilization. Without looking back and with no idea what the future held, especially without Maya in it, Peter raced to find his loved ones. He had no idea the fate of the others, but Peter did know what needed to be done. Together, they had to rebuild what was once destroyed and make the world a better place.

ONE YEAR LATER

Huddled together on the grounds of Hofstra University in a dormitory room on campus, the group listened intently as the recently appointed President, Amanda Caputo, spoke her first radio broadcast.

'My dear fellow Americans of the United States of New America...'

Hearing the United States with New in the format would take some time to get used to. In order to start anew, the country had banned together and a vote was taken by every remaining citizen to rename America. What had transpired over the course of the last twelve months in rebuilding the ruined fifty states consumed every living person. Adding the simple word of 'New' seemed to appease everyone. To change the whole country that was in existence since the year 1776 would be an injustice. Prior to 1776 it was the United Colonies and going back would add to the anxiety of what once was and could never be repeated. 'New' would make America strong again and this is what Americans now strived for. Television had still not been restored as satellite dishes were destroyed in the midst of the country falling apart. Television networks were shut down during the outbreak due to the continued loss of daily life. They had stopped televising all programming of any variety of information. News programs had lost many valuable lives and newspapers were no longer printed. A primal feeling had overtaken the country, as if prehistoric times once again ruled the earth. It had come down to survival of the fittest and anyone over the age of sixty was sacrificed regardless of their health. A vast amount of people who had been in hiding due to not being vaccinated were over the age of sixty but had yet to be accounted for. People were still afraid and unsure if it was wise or safe for them to expose themselves while still feeling vulnerable. Of the 340 million Americans that lived prior to the Rapid X Virus, that along with what Doctor Anglim did, only 197 million Americans survived. Of the 7 billion worldwide, only 3.8 billion people remained. Baby steps were needed to get the country to a place where society would be able to function the way it used to, and it would take years to get the country up and running again. Mass chaos among rioters, who no longer cared or feared that their lives would be taken from them, destroyed most metropolises. Looters overtook major cities, stealing items that would have been of no use to them regardless. The country was totally destroyed. President Caputo continued, 'And I implore each and every American citizen to come forward so we can account for you. Until we are able to rebuild each state from the impact of its destruction, only certain assigned states will take precedence over the other smaller states in total ruins. I urge each and every remaining citizen to ban together with your fellow neighbors and together we will REBUILD!'

Communities in the once overpopulated states such as Texas, California, Florida, Illinois, New York and a dozen others were set up as 'go to zones.' Thousands of families, relocated to these areas. There were plenty of housing communities to accommodate the huge numbers that were occupying them. The National Guard had been placed as added protection to these communities until police precincts were back in force. Every available space that could house people was put to use. Colleges, military bases, malls, and even factories were now new areas to settle in. People were urged to abandon their homes until law and order were back in place. While tragedy struck first with the virus and then the deadly vaccine, gangs of ruthless people roamed the country taking what was not rightfully theirs. It was like an episode from '*The Walking Dead*' without the zombies. In her conclusion President Caputo stated, 'I promise each and every living individual that we will survive, and we will come out on top. We will make NEW AMERICA strong again! What had happened will never happen again, not in this lifetime or any future lifetime. Putting our trust in one sick scientist could have wiped out the entire world. Let us not lose our focus on what is good and will remain to be good going forward. My fellow Americans, let us rebuild and let us remain with the freedom we once had. My new mantra is simply this, 'To be alive and feeling free.' We shall reign supreme from this day forward. God bless us all.'

Sitting around the radio and listening to the Presidents final words, Tommy stood up and shut it off. He then looked at the six others who were glued to the broadcast as much as he was. "I believe if anyone can get this country on its feet, it's her. She's strong willed and determined. Exactly what this country needs. She won't take shit from anyone or anything."

Melanie, who was just days away from her due date, stood up slowly while holding her stomach. "Let's just hope it sooner rather than later. I want our baby in a world like it once was."

Tommy smiled and patted her belly, "Geez, maybe you should run for office. Actually, you should be her Vice-President. You two together would really kick ass in getting New America back on track." Rita, who was now the legal guardian to Myleka as well as Linh and Khang, laughed at the absurdity of it all. In her final promise to Laureen, she was upholding her part of the last second dying request made upon her. Myleka, who was still adjusting to her mother's untimely death, would still wake up screaming in the middle of the night from reliving the ordeal. Rita was certain this would go on for quite some time. It was just Laureen and Myleka as one for years. Rita would be there through every step of Myleka's recovery for as long as it would take. Although the loss would always remain, Rita would never stop loving this girl who now held a special place in her heart. She knew she could never replace Laureen as her mother, but she would love her like no other.

Linh and Khang were inseparable more so than they once were. They never were out of each other's field of vision. The courts, which were slowly reopening, awarded Rita as their legal guardian which brought more joy to the two still insecure siblings. Surviving what they went through set them back more than one could have imagined. Rita willed herself that they would be okay as far as she was concerned. By fulfilling these requests and promises, it would enable her to slowly make peace from the loss of Nick, who took a large piece of her heart with him when he died. Rita knew she would never find a love like theirs again.

Upon the sudden realization that both of Melanies parents would no longer be in her daily life, Melanie was left with a complete emptiness. For the first few weeks she was unable to stop crying and barely ate. Lack of sleep and appetite had the newly formed family very concerned for her well-being. The heartache was too much and if not for Tommy's constant support and never leaving her side, Melanie would have given up. Each passing day spent with Tommy softened the eternal ache within her heart, and it wasn't until he proposed to her three months after their initial meeting that she had renewed purpose in life. The very first time they made love as husband and wife, Melanie became pregnant. Rita felt as if God intervened to continue to provide her daughter-in-law with new beginnings to help put both painful losses to a peaceful rest.

"So, have you two lovebirds decided on any names for the baby?" Rita inquired.

Melanie looked at Tommy and put her finger to her lips. "We do have one or two picked out. We don't want to spoil the surprise since it's any day now, but we will definitely be encompassing either my parents or your husband's name as part. You'll just have to be patient and wait and see!"

Rita seemed content with this and smiled in response.

Peter hadn't been listening to a word that any of them had spoken. Instead, he stared off into space with another matter weighing heavily on him. In less than an hour, he would be meeting a family who had lost just as much as he. Maya's family would be arriving into the country for the first time since this whole ordeal began. Major airports such as LAX, JFK, Dallas- Fort Worth International Airport, Miami International and O'Hare International Airports had reopened just the past week under the supervision of Four Star General Fernandez, of the Marine Intelligence Corps. With his clearance, major airports finally allowed families that were left stranded in other countries to make their way home. Peter, who saved the world with the vaccine that was administered to as many people world-wide as possible, was given priority on any favor he requested. He decided he was going to give Maya the proper memorial that she deserved. Even with limited cell-phone usage still available, he was able to get a text to the American embassy in Bermuda that was then personally delivered to her family. The decision to come to the states was an easy one for Maya's family as Bermuda was in ruins. They were on the first flight to John F. Kennedy International Airport in Queens. Exactly one month after the evil doctor's fall to his death, Peter and his new family of seven (soon to be eight including himself and the new baby) were transported by a military escort from Nevada to Long Island, New York by careful instructions from General Fernandez. They were then set up in a few dorm rooms at Hofstra University since their home had been set on fire by Tommy and the neighborhood now deemed unsafe as well. In the weeks that followed their return to Long Island, Peter worked closely with the newly appointed CDC scientist, Amil Badoolah. Together, they were able to duplicate the vaccine and worked with Pfizer to ensure that mass production of future vaccines were being made. In short, within three years every living being worldwide would be fully vaccinated to fight any deadly disease that they may one day face again. This could once again present a problem to those still against vaccinations, but over time hopefully they would see the benefit. Doctor Badoolah played an integral part in ensuring this. Peter was offered a prominent position within the CDC which he politely declined. After everything he had believed to be beneficial in his early career with Doctor Anglim compared to the actual truth, Peter wanted to stay clear of the scientific field for now. His main objective was to give Maya a proper service for such a short life that she lived. All of his future looked uncertain now, as his main plans always consisted of the two of them together. Peter headed to the bathroom for one last look in the mirror to make sure he was presentable. He then grabbed the sport jacket he laid out on his bed that morning and put it on. Peter glanced at the clock on the wall and noticed it was exactly twelve noon. In the past, noon had represented death by the hands of the evil doctor. Today, it took on a new positive meaning. The car service that General Fernandez sent to pick up the Burgess family had just pulled up in front of the campus where they were residing. Peter, with his mother by his side for emotional support, went to greet them. Tommy and Melanie followed behind. Linh, Khang and Myleka stayed inside eagerly awaiting to meet Maya's younger siblings. Peter stood at the entrance to the dorms and watched as two National guards approached the Ford Escalade. One of the guards opened the front passenger door as the other proceeded to do the same for the passengers. Maya's father stepped out of the front seat and took hold of his wife's hand as she came out of the car. Even from a distance, Peter surmised that tears had been shed by Maya's mother as she dabbed at her eyes with a handkerchief. Her husband gently placed his hand on her elbow and moved in the general direction toward him. Next came the two youngest of the family. The brother appeared to be in his early twenties, while if his memory served him correctly, the sister was almost twenty. Both of them appeared solemn, too. The loss of their daughter and sister weighed heavily upon the whole family. Peter tried to remember the last time he saw them. It had been quite some time since he did. Then, as if it happened in slow motion, the last child slowly made her way out of the Escalade. Her slender legs appeared first, followed by the rest of her body. As she straightened herself out, she tossed back her full mane of hair. Peter blinked and then blinked again. The similarity was uncanny. The looks on his mom's face as well as his brothers confirmed exactly what he was seeing right before his eyes. Maya was ALIVE! Somehow she survived the fall into the rushing waters from the dam. She made it safely back to her family and here she was alive and in the flesh, and now she had come to reclaim their lives together. Like a fairytale ending, they would live happily ever after. Peter lost his grip on reality and was beyond elated. In his haste, he rushed past Maya's parents and her two youngest siblings without acknowledging them. He wanted to lift her in his arms and spin her around until they both tumbled to the ground in a fit of laughter. Peter was inches away from her. Suddenly, he stopped dead in his tracks when he saw panic in the eyes of his one true love. Rushing towards her must have somehow scared her. Now, having come to a complete halt, he stopped mid- sentence from proclaiming his undying love for her. "Maya, Oh God... Maya! Is it really you?" Peter rubbed his eyes to make sure. "How can it be? I saw you fall from the helicopter with my own two eyes." Again, Peter took a double take. He spoke fast and babbled. "Why didn't you call? I mean after all this time, why wouldn't you call me and tell me you were ALIVE?" Before he could ask any more questions, he was silenced when her finger touched his lips. Delicately and with as much compassion as possible, Maya's image answered, "Oh my Lord. You must have forgotten with all the pressure you've been under this past year. I'm so sorry Peter. Truly I am. But I'm not Maya. I'm really not. I'm her identical twin, Kayla. Please forgive me. I didn't realize the affect it would have on you. We should have known. All of us should have. We should have prepared you for this. I'm so SO SORRY!"

Peter couldn't believe what he was hearing. He tried to block it out but couldn't. Standing before him wasn't his one true love. In Maya's place was her identical twin sister, Kayla. Maya always talked about how much they were alike. They had the same taste in food, music and just about everything else. She missed her most when her family moved to Bermuda. Maya was so used to sharing every life experience with her twin and often found it difficult when they weren't face to face. This saddened her immensely and she often had sudden outbursts of tears from her identical twin's absence. With this realization, it all came back to Peter as one big blow. After all he had been through, this was his most devastating reality check yet. A knife straight through his heart shattering every ounce of hope he had left.

Once again he had lost the love of his life. Now, Kayla would be a constant reminder of the girl he could never spend or share his life together with as one. Ironically, Maya's family planned on staying nearby for the imminent future, but Maya wouldn't be with any of them. That girl died when she fell from the helicopter. This was all too much to take in as Peter dropped to his knees. He then cried and cried until he couldn't shed another tear. The others looked on and let him be. There would be ample time to offer love and support. Peter closed his eyes. He then put his face in his hands and didn't want to ever open them again. His thoughts at the moment were baffling. He knew he would have to face them sooner or later if he could muster the strength and courage. Life as Peter knew it would restore itself to a new beginning for all of humanity. His life, however, once again ended for all of eternity, an eternity that would continue to haunt him each and every time he saw Kayla's face.

Thank you so much for reading and I hope you enjoyed it! I would truly appreciate you leaving a quick review on Amazon. If you'd like to reach out to me my links are below:

www.facebook.com/vincentscialobooks
vscialo@gmail.com

This is Vincent N. Scialo's ninth and most thrilling novel to date. Unlike his previous eight novels this book touches on an actual occurrence that recently swept the world. The realization of the pandemic hit close to home for every living breathing person. His novels The Rocking Chair and Randolph's Tale (A Journey for Love) still receive much acclaim and are still showcased at the Washington D.C. Holocaust Museum. They are still his most talked about books. For those who crave the ultimate in horror and suspense, a taste of Deep in the Woods will leave you sleeping with the lights on. And if you ever wondered what lives the seven little men led before meeting the purest of snow, Vincent offers a dark fabled fairytale. Heigh-Ho is for the young at heart still in love with classic bed-time stories. Not by Choice will grip you from start to finish as his medical suspense has the reader rooting for the main character throughout the story. For those spiritually enlightened, JESUS (Journey every step un-sure) lets you experience what it would be like to walk the four seasons with Jesus at your side. For the reader faint at heart, The Decision leaves you praying the three couples make the right choice and survive the outcome. A Final Destination meets A Simple Plan.

On a lighter note Vincent tried his hand at his first children's book inspired by his granddaughter Emma. The Many Adventures of Grandpa and Grandpa's Girl takes you on four different life lessons that only a grandpa can explain in fun-filled descriptions.

Vincent continues to perfect his work while residing in Bellmore, Long Island with his wife Jennifer. Their son, Jeff, recently moved to Raleigh, North Carolina to expand his Kettlecorn business. His daughter Marissa, her husband Harry and his two granddaughters Stephanie and Emma live close by in Massapequa providing him with as much family time when needed.